"A sensitive storyteller who always touches readers' hearts." —*Romantic Times*

Praise for the novels of Cassie Edwards

"High adventure and a surprise season this Indian romance." —*Affaire de Coeur*

"Edwards puts an emphasis on placing authentic customs and language in each book. Her Indian books have generated much interest throughout the country, and elsewhere." —*Journal-Gazette* (Mattoon, IL)

"Edwards consistently gives the reader a strong love story, rich in Indian lore, filled with passion and memorable characters." —*Romantic Times*

"A fine writer . . . and language kee[ps] . . ." —(CO)

"Excellent . . . a . . . filled with heart-warming c[haracters]" —*Under the Covers*

"Captivating . . . heartwarming . . . beautiful . . . a winner." —*Rendezvous*

"Edwards moves readers with love and compassion." —*Bell, Book & Candle*

Also by Cassie Edwards

NIGHT
WOLF

Cassie Edwards

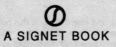

A SIGNET BOOK

SIGNET
Published by New American Library, a division of
Penguin Group (USA) Inc., 375 Hudson Street,
New York, New York 10014, U.S.A.
Penguin Books Ltd, 80 Strand,
London WC2R 0RL, England
Penguin Books Australia Ltd, 250 Camberwell Road,
Camberwell, Victoria 3124, Australia
Penguin Books Canada Ltd, 10 Alcorn Avenue,
Toronto, Ontario, Canada M4V 3B2
Penguin Books (N.Z.) Ltd, Cnr Rosedale and Airborne Roads,
Albany, Auckland 1310, New Zealand

Penguin Books Ltd Registered Offices:
80 Strand, London WC2R 0RL, England

First published by Signet, an imprint of New American Library,
a division of Penguin Group (USA) Inc.

First Printing, December 2003
10 9 8 7 6 5 4 3 2 1

PUBLISHER'S NOTE
This is a work of fiction. Names, characters, places, and incidents either are the
product of the author's imagination or are used fictitiously, and any resemblance to actual persons, living or dead, business establishments, events or lo-
cales is entirely coincidental.

In love and friendship, I dedicate *Night Wolf* to my dear friends Lee and Bill Bell, and to the cast and crew of their television shows *The Bold and the Beautiful* and *The Young and the Restless*—especially sweet Camryn Grimes, who portrays "Cassie."

"Shadow of My Love"

I watch through the corner of my eye
As your shadow goes dancing by.
I smell your scent, I need your touch,
I want to hold you, oh, so much.
The world says we can never be,
I say you are the only one for me.
So . . . we will join our hearts together,
For today, tomorrow, now, and forever.
We will look past the difference of our skin,
And a new life together we will begin!

—Diane Collett, poet and friend

Chapter 1

Montana Territory—1846
Penahque-geezis—Moon of Falling Leaves

In the afternoon shadow of a large, cone-shaped tepee, the young chief of the Cree tribe stood before a group of his braves. He was dressed in fringed buckskin, his waist-length, coal-black hair hanging smooth and sleek down his straight back and his jet-black eyes leveling a lingering gaze at each of the braves.

"Young braves, what you have done disappoints this chief very much," Night Wolf said, his arms folded tightly across his chest. "What you did was *mah-nah-dud*, bad. You have degraded yourselves, even your people, over what you chose to steal beneath the light of the moon. It is a thing of pride to steal horses. But the white man's potatoes? Do you truly see pride in stealing food from the mouths of the elderly black-robed priests at the mission? Do you feel brave and strong for having done it? Do you . . . feel . . . proud?"

When none of the group seemed ready to apologize or explain their actions, Night Wolf again looked from one to the other. "Young braves, you who are the future of our Cree people, does not our world of forests, prairies, mountains, rivers, and skies give you everything you need?" he asked. "Does it not provide you food, shelter, clothing, and life itself?"

The boys nodded.

"Young braves, those things I just spoke of were not stolen—they were gifts from *Wenebojo*, the Great Spirit," he continued. "These black-robed holy men are living from the soil because they are too old for the hunt, so can you not see how wrong it is to take food from them?"

Two Wings, the mastermind of the thievery, who had led his friends into doing it, smiled weakly up at Night Wolf. "My chief, we did this not for ourselves but for our mothers," he said in a voice that was just beginning to change from a child's into a young man's. It would be steady, then would suddenly crack and sink to a lower pitch. "My chief, since Father Mulvaney introduced our people to this food one moon ago, our mothers have longed for more of it to put into their cook pots but have not asked the priest for it."

Another of the braves, called Long Nose because his nose was longer than those of most Cree, stepped closer to Two Wings and spoke his piece. "My chief, do you not see that if our *gee-mah-mah*s have potatoes for their cook pots, then they will not need to bend their backs to dig roots and bulbs that grow wild on the land? Because of wanting to help our mothers in this way, we saw no wrong in taking the potatoes for them. Do not Mother Earth and what grows in it belong to *all* people?"

Night Wolf sighed heavily. "*Gah-ween*, no," he said. "Not if what is in the ground came from seeds purposely placed there by a particular person for his food."

He shook his head, then looked intently at each brave in turn. "It was wrong, especially, to steal from the black-robes, who have only peace and love in their hearts," he said. "Although the Cree have not accepted the *chee-mo-ko-man*'s God, the Cree have affection for the kind old men who worship their God with love and adulation just as the Cree worship their own Great Spirit."

"I understand now," Two Wings replied. He humbly hung his head. "My chief, my heart feels *ah-gah-dayn-dush-mo-win*. I apologize."

The others soon followed his lead with heads bowed in shame.

"Young braves, it is good that you finally see the error of your ways," Night Wolf said, nodding at the boys. He unfolded his arms and placed a hand on first one brave's shoulder, and then another until he had given each of them reason to know that he lovingly accepted the apologies.

"But now you have more to do with that apology," he said. They suddenly looked at him with wary questioning in their eyes. "It is required now for you all to go to Father Mulvaney and not only apologize to him personally but also take the stolen property back to him."

They exchanged troubled glances, then looked to their chief and nodded.

"But first you must go and admit what you have done to your parents, ask for their forgiveness, as well as pray for the same to *Wenebojo*. Then meet me in the council house," Night Wolf said. "I will escort you to the mission."

The boys left him, running in different directions to their tepees. Night Wolf turned and walked toward his mother's dwelling, which sat not far from Night Wolf's much larger one.

Since he would be going to the mission

today, he decided to give the journey a dual purpose. Recently a trading post had been built between the mission and Fort Harris. Night Wolf had yet to meet the man in charge at the trading post, but he knew his name was Trader Joe. Night Wolf would go there and make his acquaintance.

Until now, Night Wolf and his people had always been forced to travel far to a trading post, so they were glad that this one had been established closer to their village.

The autumn winds were blowing and winter was almost upon them. Most of his people's supplies were in and ready for the winter. Their hunt had been good and would last them until the spring. But Night Wolf had a few pelts left to take to this new trading post.

His main reason for going, though, was to assess the post's worth. And to assess the man who owned it. This was best done before the spring buffalo hunt, as he wanted to be able to lead his warriors to the right trading post so that they could achieve the best trade.

When Night Wolf reached his mother's tepee, he entered and stood just inside. He gazed down at his mother as she worked on her beading beside a warm fire.

It tugged at his heart to realize how quickly she had aged since losing her husband four moons ago. He had been killed during a buffalo hunt when he had dared an old bull one time too many.

It pained Night Wolf to see his mother's furrowed face and gray hair. Her eyes and cheeks were sunken, and her sallow skin lay thin upon her pinched nose and high cheekbones. She wore her hair tightly braided atop her head and had wrapped a red blanket around her crossed legs. The loose sleeve of her doeskin dress revealed a thin wrist with many silver bracelets.

Sensing his presence, Yellow Blossom stopped her beading and smiled up at him. "My son, what brings you to my lodge with such a downtrodden look?" she asked in a feeble voice. "*Mah-bee-szhon*, come. Sit with your mother. Tell her what is on your mind."

Nodding and smiling, Night Wolf went and sat beside her on the thick pallet of furs. He leaned forward and lifted a piece of wood into the flames of the fire, then turned to her. "*Gee-mah-mah*, Mother, I have to accompany some of the young braves to the mission today," he said. "They are returning stolen property."

"Stolen property?" his mother repeated, raising an eyebrow. "What sort?"

"In the night they went and dug potatoes from the mission garden," he told her. "They now know the wrong that they did, and they are returning the potatoes, and with them their heartfelt apologies."

"Shame on them for taking what was not theirs," Yellow Blossom said, sighing. She gazed upon her son, a man of honor who would never take anything that was not his. Instead, he was one of the most generous gift *givers*, especially to the toothless old people of their village.

For his goodness and his honesty, and for being the chief of their Wolf band of Cree people, a chief who both led and protected, he was entitled to the red-painted smoke lapels on his tepee, a sign granted only to men of honor.

Yellow Blossom also saw his handsomeness and his noble countenance. He was a man of intelligence, a man who made friends easily.

This helped him greatly in his dealings with those who ran the trading posts. Because of who he was, and how he used his intelligence, he could make deals for his furs that no others could make. His skill benefited his Cree people, so much so that they rarely wanted for anything. If they needed it, Night Wolf made certain they received it.

Yellow Blossom's heart was warmed every time her son came and sat with her and kept her company, for she had been so lonely since the death of her beloved husband.

"The young braves did not see the wrong in taking from the earth since they have been taught that what is in the earth is there for the taking and has even been placed there for the good of our people," Night Wolf said. "I had to explain that taking what grows naturally from the earth is different from taking what someone else has planted."

"And they understood?" Yellow Blossom asked, resuming her needlework as she slowly sewed more beads onto a buckskin vest that she had made for her son.

"*Ay-uh*, yes, I believe so," Night Wolf said, nodding. He watched his mother's fingers laboring with each bead. He knew that each painful movement was a labor of love, for she was making something special for him.

"*Gee-mah-mah*, while I am at the mission I plan to also go and make acquaintance at the new trading post," he said. "The *chee-mo-ko-man* in charge is called by the name Trader Joe. It is good to make friends with him now so that when spring comes, trading with him will be done with more ease. Mother, I know that you have everything you need for the long winter months ahead. Is there something else at the

8

trading post that you might want? Is there anything special that I can get for you?"

Again Yellow Blossom paused in her beading. She squinted her eyes in thought, then smiled at Night Wolf. "*Ay-uh*, yes, my son, I would like some red cloth and white woman's buttons—pearl, I believe they are called," she said. "Also some marbles for my grandson, Little Moon."

She smiled and a look of pride came to her eyes. "Ah, that grandson of mine. It seems only yesterday that your sister, Moon Song, held him in her arms after he came from the comforting warmth of her womb. Now he is five winters of age and growing so quickly into a young brave."

"He *is* growing quickly, and he enjoys challenges of a child of ten," Night Wolf said, as in his mind's eye he saw his long-legged nephew with his flowing hair and mischievous black eyes. "Marbles are his favorite challenge. Yes, I shall get him several."

"Get him the ones with the brightest colors," Yellow Blossom said, her eyes smiling into Night Wolf's.

"*Gee-mah-mah*, I believe you enjoy looking at the marbles even more than Little Moon enjoys using them for challenges," Night Wolf said, chuckling.

"*Ay-uh*, they are something pretty to look at and to hold," Yellow Blossom said, herself laughing in a low sort of cackle.

"I will do these things for you," Night Wolf said. "Is there anything else that you can think of?"

"Yes, will you find something special, a surprise, for our friend Shame on Face?" Yellow Blossom said, resuming her work. "Find something special for her. She needs some sunshine in her life." She frowned. "I do wish that she would not stay so much to herself."

Night Wolf nodded as he thought of Shame on Face. The woman of whom his mother spoke had lived alone, childless and husbandless, since she had given birth to a baby eighteen winters ago. Because of the shame of carrying the child that was not her husband's, she gave herself the name Shame on Face.

Only Night Wolf and his mother visited the self-shamed woman; otherwise she was all alone. She rarely left her lodge. Everyone knew of her illicit affair, but only she knew whose baby she had carried inside her womb. She never spoke of it to anyone, not even her best friend, Yellow Blossom.

Everyone knew the child was not her husband's, for a wound inflicted on him during a skirmish with the Blackfoot had made it impossible for him to have a child with his wife. When he had seen her belly swollen with child, he had left her and the village, and no one had seen him since.

She had carried the child to full term. One day she walked out of the village big with child and returned that night, her belly flat. No one knew what she did with the newborn child and no one asked. It was her affair . . . her child.

Being Chippewa, Shame on Face would have returned to her true people far away in the land of many lakes, but her friend Yellow Blossom had said the journey was too long back to Minnesota country, too taxing and dangerous a trip for a woman. Yellow Blossom had told her friend that she would miss her terribly. She promised Shame on Face that she and Night Wolf would be there for her always.

Because of all of those things, Shame on Face had stayed, and through his mother's love and understanding for the woman, Night Wolf had learned to love and not to condemn Shame on Face, to help her with whatever needs she might have.

"Son, you choose her surprise gift, for you love her as much as I," Yellow Blossom said.

Night Wolf gave her a kiss, then rose to his feet. "*Ay-uh*, I shall bring something special for Shame on Face," he said. His gaze shifted to the vest. "*Gee-mah-mah*, you still bead with such skill. It is good that you wish to keep your hands busy in such a way."

"I enjoy it as much now as I did many moons ago, perhaps even more," Yellow Blossom said, holding the vest out, admiring it herself. "It does these old fingers good to keep them active."

"I shall not be gone for too long," Night Wolf said. He smiled one last time at her, then stepped out into the afternoon sunshine. As he walked toward the council house, he stopped before Shame on Face's tepee. He saw the darkness of the buffalo hides, the dirtiness of them. Since her husband's abandonment of her those long years ago, she had never renewed her lodge, which all women did every spring. The tail ends were in shreds, and the hides were streaked from smoke and age. Many times he had offered to wrap new hides around her lodgepoles, even to erect her a new lodge, but she had refused and said that living in this way was also a part of her shame.

His mother came once a year and did her best to sew the shredded ends together. Shame on Face at least allowed that.

Night Wolf went on and into the council house, where the young braves awaited him.

Soon they were all on their way to the mission, he on his magnificent strawberry roan, they on their ponies. Two Wings carried the bag of shame, the potatoes, on his horse.

Night Wolf carried enough pelts tied to the back of his steed for trading at the new trading post. He always looked forward to meeting new people, to see whether or not they held trust in their eyes and friendship in their handshake. With whites, one never knew what to expect. Night Wolf knew from experience that many were untrustworthy and conniving. For his people's sake, since this trading post was so close to their village downriver, he hoped that Trader Joe would hold none of those ugly traits.

Chapter 2

The earth had been upturned, leaving gaps in the ground where one long row of potatoes had been dug up and taken. Marissa McHugh stood with Father Mulvaney staring at the obvious proof of someone's thievery.

"How horrible," Marissa murmured, turning to the black-robed priest. He was a gray-haired man in his early seventies whose face had a godly peace to it. His smile was always warm and friendly.

"Who could have done this?" she asked. "Who would steal from priests?"

Father Mulvaney sighed heavily and looked sadly at Marissa. He had instantly been taken by her loveliness the very first time he had seen her. She had long, thick, coal-black hair that framed her oval face and beautifully shaped full lips. Her wide, vivacious violet eyes would capture any young man's heart.

He smiled even now as he recalled that his

beloved mother's nose had had the same slightly upturned end as Marissa's, with a scattering of freckles across it.

Yes, he knew that what truly had captured his attention *was* Marissa's resemblance to his mother, who had gone to meet her Master too many years ago, leaving a void in his heart that he had filled by spreading and teaching the Gospel to those who needed God's nourishment.

Even though his mission was only built from logs, he was proud of it and of the wooden cross made by his friend Night Wolf after Father Mulvaney had explained the importance of having a cross to identify the building as a mission rather than a trading post or a settler's cabin.

Night Wolf had felt comfortable helping the priests. Father Mulvaney had vowed that neither he nor any of the other priests at his mission would try to persuade the Cree people to choose the priests' God over their own. Father Mulvaney would, indeed, like to try, but he had assured Night Wolf that he was there for whites only. And Father Mulvaney never broke a promise.

He had established his mission close to Fort Harris so that those who resided there would have a place to worship. And now there was the new trading post, which would draw settlers who might also seek out the comforting arms of the mission.

The trading post had been there for only a month. Marissa's father, Joseph, who was called Trader Joe by many who knew him, had been the one to bring the establishment to this Territory. The trading post was well stocked with supplies that he had brought from Kansas. He had told Father Mulvaney that he arrived early so he could establish the trading post before the onset of winter and so that the post would be ready for spring trade with the Indians after their successful buffalo hunt.

Marissa had confided to Father Mulvaney that she loved this new land already—its wildness and its endless blue sky. To the priest, Marissa was like a breath of fresh air. He looked forward to all time spent with her.

"Who would do this?" she asked him now, her gaze moving down the long row of upturned earth. "Who stole the potatoes?"

"I believe it could be the work of some young, mischievous braves from the Cree village," answered Father Mulvaney.

"The Cree?" Marissa said. She looked to her left, where the river rumbled not that far from her father's trading post. He had built it up on a slight hill from the river in case the banks overflowed in the spring, when the snows melted from the mountaintops and rushed down into the river below. "Father has talked of the Cree, but thus far I have yet to see any."

She turned back to Father Mulvaney. "I have eagerly waited to see the Indians, yet none have come," she said. "Do you think they might be going to another trading post for their supplies?"

"It has been only a month since your father opened the doors of his trading post," Father Mulvaney said, stooping to run his fingers through the upturned dirt. "I imagine some Cree will come for last-minute supplies before the harsh weather keeps them inside their lodges. But they probably won't have a need to do a lot of trading. From what I know of them, they already went to the trading post farther downriver that they used for many years. They do not wait for the bad weather to come before they ready themselves for it. I'm certain they are already prepared for the first spattering of snow."

"You said that you believe that the ones who stole the potatoes from you are the Cree," Marissa said, stooping down beside Father Mulvaney. She too, ran her fingers through the rich soil. "If the Cree are so efficient at getting in their supplies for the winter, why would braves feel a need to steal potatoes?"

"I have no idea, unless it was done for mischief's sake alone," Father Mulvaney said. "The sad thing about this is that this year there is an overabundance of potatoes, way too many for the supper tables at both the fort and my mission. I had planned to offer you and your father some and then take what was left to the Cree village. I wanted to show them how to plant them so that they could have their own potatoes next year."

Marissa started to say something, then stopped when she heard the sound of approaching horses. She turned and saw a warrior on horseback followed by six young braves on ponies.

"I believe those who stole from me are arriving even now," Father Mulvaney said. He shaded his eyes from the sun as he watched them approach. "Yes, that's Night Wolf, the Cree chief, and those are the braves from his village. I can tell their purpose for being here by their behavior, by how their heads are hung in shame. Do you see the bag on the one young brave's pony? In that bag are more than likely my potatoes. Yes, the guilty ones are returning what they stole."

Marissa scarcely heard what Father Mulvaney was saying. Instead, her eyes were on the warrior who sat tall in his saddle, his chin lifted high, his jet-black eyes glittering.

Never had she seen such a handsome man as this Chief Night Wolf. He wore a fringed, smoke-tanned buckskin shirt, decorated with green porcupine quillwork. His leggings and moccasins were of the same color as his shirt. He wore a single eagle feather upright at the back of his head, a knife at his belt. He was uniquely attractive, with a look of controlled power.

As he saw her standing there beside Father Mulvaney, the expression in his dark eyes changed to a questioning wonder.

With his eyes on her now, slowly sweeping from her head to her toes, Marissa suddenly felt weak-kneed. She felt a strange flip-flopping sensation at the pit of her stomach. All of these feelings were new to her, and she realized that for the first time in her life she was attracted to a man. And this was not just any man. He was an Indian!

The sight of him made Marissa's breath catch in her throat.

Back in Kansas, she had been kept from Indians who came to the river to trade. But here, where Indians outnumbered whites, and where her father had set up trade with them, she had known that she would get the opportunity to meet some, eye to eye. She had wondered about what sort of chief they would have. Now she knew, and she was awed by him.

With a rapid heartbeat she watched the warrior getting closer and closer. She edged over next to Father Mulvaney.

"You said that the older one is a chief?" she said, realizing that Night Wolf was still looking at her.

She wondered what he was thinking. Did he like what he saw? Or did he resent her being here, as most redskins resented whites who came to land that had at one time been solely the red man's?

Surely once he realized that she was not just an ordinary settler but instead the daughter of the man who owned the new trading post, which had been established there solely for the good of the Indians, he would see her as a friend and might—might—even one day take the time to talk with her.

The very thought of that made her heart skip a couple of beats. Then its thundering resumed inside her chest.

"Yes, he is his people's chief," Father Mulvaney said, lifting a hand to greet Night Wolf, who returned the wave. "He is Night Wolf, of the Wolf band of the Cree tribe. Their village is downriver a piece. They are a friendly people. I especially like and admire Night Wolf. He is a young chief, a peaceful and good man."

They had no time to say anything else, since Night Wolf drew a tight rein a few feet away and dismounted. Marissa felt swallowed whole now by her heartbeats as Night Wolf stood before Father Mulvaney and placed a gentle hand on the priest's shoulder.

"My friend, it is good to see you again, but the reason for my visit this time is not a good one," Night Wolf said. He lowered his hand to his side, turned and gazed at the young braves, who were still on their ponies, their heads hung in their shame.

Then he looked at Father Mulvaney again. "I have brought these young braves with me today for a purpose that saddens my heart," he said. "They came like thieves in the night and stole from you." He looked at the upturned earth and sighed. "I see that you have discovered the thievery. My friend, the young braves have come with what they stole, and with apologies for their ill behavior."

Although Night Wolf was there to make things right with Father Mulvaney, he could not help but slide his gaze over to the woman who stood at the black-robe's side. While arriving on his steed, he had seen the woman, and at first sight, he realized that there was something special about her. He knew people well. He could read their personalities in their eyes, and what he had seen—what he was even now seeing in this woman's eyes—told him that she was someone he would know better, someone he *must* know better.

It was not that he was taken by her sweet prettiness, by her lovely, *ah-gah-sah*, petite, yet deliciously curved body. Although he did see her as *mee-kah-wah-diz-ee*, beautiful, it was something else, but he could not figure out what it was.

He forced his thoughts back to where they should be, and his eyes as well, as he centered his attention once again on Father Mulvaney and the problem at hand.

"My son, do not fret so much over what the young braves did," Father Mulvaney said in a compassionate voice. "It is only a few potatoes. But I do understand your concern. Stealing is wrong, no matter the age of those who are guilty of doing it."

"My young people, boys and girls alike, are taught the wrong in taking what is not theirs from the moment they have the logic of understanding right from wrong," Night Wolf said.

He looked over his shoulder at the young

braves, then at Father Mulvaney again. "They will apologize to you for their shame, and when they return home, they will face their punishment," he said.

"I understand your need to punish those who have done wrong, Night Wolf, yet I have already forgiven the young braves," Father Mulvaney said. He looked past Night Wolf and smiled. He could tell that his words had reached the ears of the young braves by the way their heads jerked up. They were now smiling at him from ear to ear.

"*But*—" Father Mulvaney said, noticing how that one word, and the way he said it, erased the smiles. "But if you feel that they need to be punished, they can be put to work digging up the other potatoes alongside me and the other priests who plan to dig today."

He smiled to himself when he saw more than one of the boys heave a sigh of relief, for they knew, as did he, that this punishment was nothing like what they had thought it might be. They were getting off easy for their wrongdoing, and they knew it.

He was being clever himself, doing this in hopes of bringing the children closer to the Lord, but he would never admit that to anyone. He did not want to say or do anything to cause a strain between himself and Night Wolf and his people. Thus far, he had been careful not to preach his religion to them. He had hoped that in time they would come to him and question him about it. Only then would he openly bring it to them. Only then . . .

"I see that plan as good. *Mee-gway-chee-wahn-dum*, thank you," Night Wolf replied.

Again his eyes shifted to the woman, and he found her eyes on him as well.

Father Mulvaney noticed how Night Wolf and Marissa were quietly observing one another.

"Night Wolf, this is Marissa McHugh. Marissa, this is Night Wolf," Father Mulvaney said, smiling at both of them.

"It is good to meet you," Marissa said, clumsily reaching a hand out toward Night Wolf, unsure if that was the thing to do when she met an Indian face-to-face, eye to eye.

Seeing her extended hand, and understanding this was the way white people showed an appreciation of meeting someone, Night Wolf reached a hand out for hers.

He felt the softness of her flesh against his. Already attracted by her voice, which was like a sweet song, so soft and lyrical, he felt a strange yearning that was new to him. Something in his heart spoke to him, saying that this woman was different, for never had any woman made him react as he was now reacting to Marissa.

He started to tell her that he enjoyed meeting her, but was interrupted when the other priests from this mission arrived with bags and digging tools.

He regretfully released Marissa's hand and turned to the one short, black-robed priest, who stepped closer to him, peering up at him through thick-lensed glasses.

"Good morning, Night Wolf," Father Harbison said, then frowned when he saw the upturned earth. He looked questioningly at Father Mulvaney.

"I shall explain later," Father Mulvaney said, as the other three priests were also looking perplexed by what they saw.

Realizing that he had yet to tell his young braves the plan, although he knew that they had heard Father Mulvaney say it, Night Wolf went to them and again explained what they must do to atone for their sins.

Each of them quickly dismounted, but only one approached Father Mulvaney.

"We apologize for what we did," Two Wings said, his eyes wavering as he held the bag out to Father Mulvaney.

"As I told your chief, you are each *ah-bway-yay-nim*," Father Mulvaney said, taking the bag. He was proud to say "forgiven" in the language of the Cree.

Night Wolf had taught the priests several of his people's words. He had also explained to Father Mulvaney that he had learned the English language from his father and grandfather, who learned it from white traders when they lived in Minnesota land.

But when they were not speaking in the English language, they usually spoke Chippewa, because the Cree had become close friends with the Chippewa when they lived in the land of many lakes.

The Cree had been able to learn the Chippewa language much more quickly than the Chippewa had learned Cree. Therefore, they had mainly spoken to one another in the Chippewa language when they were together as allies and friends.

"We *mee-gway-chee-wahn-dum*, thank you, for your forgiveness," one of the other braves said, smiling broadly, realizing just how lucky they were to have such an understanding friend in Father Mulvaney. What he was asking of those who took from him was a simple enough punishment. "We will help you now. We shall dig all of the potatoes. You do not have to help."

"It will go much more quickly if we all do

our part," Father Mulvaney said, placing a hand on the young brave's shoulder.

Seeing that things were going as they should, and proud of his braves for being this willing to make up for the wrong they had done, and also feeling awkward for the first time in his life in the presence of a woman, Night Wolf went to his horse and swung into the saddle.

"I must excuse myself," he said, avoiding Marissa's eyes this time, for each time he looked at her anew he was more deeply drawn to her. "I will go now and meet the owner of the trading post—Trader Joe, I believe, is his name."

As he wheeled his horse around and started riding toward the trading post, Marissa blurted out, "Night Wolf, Trader Joe is my father!"

She blushed when he turned and gazed at her over his shoulder, then she knelt and started digging potatoes along with the young braves, who were already hard at work.

Marissa could not believe what she had done. She had never in her life been so forward with a man.

But never in her life had she been so affected by anyone as she was with Night Wolf!

Chapter 3

Smiling over how the white woman had told him that Trader Joe was her father—so bold, then becoming so *ah-gah-gee-sky*, shy, immediately afterward—Night Wolf went into the trading post. He was impressed by what he saw there. The shelves were neatly stacked with bolts of cloth, blankets of all colors, food products, and anything else one might need to get through a dreadful winter. The smell was new, clean and fresh, not like most aged trading posts that reeked of pelts that might still have the smell of blood on them. And there was glass on the front of the cabinets beneath the long counter in the room. Behind those were jars of what he now knew was candy that white people enjoyed eating. In a barrel on the floor at one end of the counter were dill pickles which white people made out of something else that was new to him—cucumbers. Curiosity had always led him to ask questions about anything new that he came across. Learning was something that Night Wolf never got enough of.

"What can I do for you?" the man called out as he came from the back rooms of the trading post, which Night Wolf assumed was also his home.

Night Wolf turned to face the man, realizing that this was surely Trader Joe—Marissa's father.

He was a huge, bulky man, with a round, rosy-cheeked face. His hair was the color of wheat and worn to his collar. He was dressed in buckskin that was lacking in fringe but was new and smelled as clean as the man himself, who brought a good smell with him when he approached and extended a hand in friendship toward Night Wolf.

"I have come for small trade today, not large," Night Wolf said, accepting the handshake as he nodded toward the loaded shelves of goods. "I am called Chief Night Wolf. I am of the Wolf band of Cree. My people's home is downriver from Fort Harris, and now also your trading post."

"I have heard of you," Joseph said, noting this chief had a grip of steel. He eased his hand away. "Father Mulvaney told me about you and your people. I hope that you will consider coming to my trading post now for all of your trade."

"You are positioned much closer to my village than any other, so, *ay-uh*, yes, I will urge my people to come here," Night Wolf said, now studying the white man's eyes and finding it strange that they were not the same color as his daughter's eyes which had mesmerized him.

Instead of being the color of violets that grew wild in the forest, this man's eyes were a strange greenish brown, changing color according to how the light from the opened door and window fell into them.

"And what have you come for today?" Joseph asked, going to stand behind the counter. He idly ran his hands along the freshly varnished top, his eyes still on Night Wolf, who seemed friendly enough.

He was used to the genteel Indians who came to the shores along Kansas City's waterfront for trade. He knew that out here in big sky country, though, there were many hostile redskins who would stop at nothing to get a white man's scalp. That was why he had urged Marissa never to ride far from the trading post and fort alone. Yet still she had, which prompted him to decide there was only one way to take that wildness out of her. He would marry her off.

He had found the right man and could hardly wait to get vows spoken between his daughter and the young man, whom even Joseph's best friend, the colonel at Fort Harris, encouraged Marissa to marry.

It had been arranged—all but getting Marissa's agreement. Joseph had been able to tell that at first glance she hadn't liked his choice, but she had known the young major for only a month. She hadn't had enough time to know him as well as the colonel, who had bragged constantly about the young soldier.

In a sense, the major was the colonel's protégé. He was eager to learn all that he must to be a colonel himself one day. He was exactly what Joseph wanted in a son-in-law, for there had once been a time when Joseph himself had aspired to such a lofty position. But things had changed quickly when he had found the bundle of joy in the forest . . .

"I have pelts to exchange for the few items I need today," Night Wolf said, drawing Joseph's attention back to him. He nodded toward the door. "They are on my steed if you would like to step to the door and see them."

"Yes, I think I will," Joseph said. He took long, lazy strides to the door. His eyes widened when he saw the plushness of the pelts that were tied to the back of the strawberry roan.

He gave Night Wolf a sidewise glance. "Mighty fine. Those are mighty fine pelts indeed," he said. "Get whatever supplies you need. We will make a good exchange."

Joseph was pleased. If this was a sample of what to expect in the future from the Cree chief and his warriors, he had come to the right place to establish his trading post.

He went back behind the counter as Night Wolf walked slowly around the huge room, taking this and that, bringing the items back and placing them on the counter.

"Yes, this post will be much handier for my people," Night Wolf said. He bent low to see a huge jar that sat on a shelf beneath the counter, in which were many colorful marbles. "My warriors will not have to carry their pelts so far next *wahbegvone-geezis*, which in my language means 'moon of the flowers,' after the successful buffalo hunt."

"I will be fair in all of my dealings with the Cree and will appreciate your business," Joseph said. "If you don't see what you want today, ask for it. By springtime I will have it for you. I shall send word to Kansas City, and it will arrive by riverboat by the time your spring hunt is over."

"That is appreciated, but today I have mainly come for supplies that will complete those that are stored already for winter, those that I could not find at the other trading post," Night Wolf said. "Too often that post does not carry an adequate supply of things needed by my people."

"I assure you that I will carry everything that you would ever ask for," Joseph said, smiling broadly. "And if I don't have it, I *will* send for it. I am here to please, Night Wolf. I am here to please."

Night Wolf's eyebrows rose at those words. He wondered if the eager-voiced *chee-mo-ko-man*, white man, truly meant that, for it was his fervent wish to know more about this man's daughter.

If he asked, would the white man supply the answers, or would he say that she was not included in his offerings?

Most white fathers deplored the very thought of a red man getting near their daughters, much less out and out asking about them.

Night Wolf knew better than to ask now. He would find a way to talk with Marissa's father about her. He wanted to know about this woman, to hear her voice again. He would never forget the first time he had heard her speak. It lay in his heart like a soft melody.

He knew it was wrong to be thinking anything about her. He had promised to marry another woman. She would soon be arriving from the Minnesota Territory with her brother, Brave Hawk, Night Wolf's best friend of long ago, when the band of Cree had neighbored with the St. Croix band of Chippewa in the land of many lakes. When he had last seen Blue Star, she had been five, he twelve.

At a meeting of tribes five moons ago, Brave Hawk had talked incessantly about his beautiful sister, Blue Star, and how he would like nothing more than to see his best friend and his sister married.

Remembering a young girl with pretty black eyes and a sweet smile, Night Wolf had agreed to marry Blue Star. He was ready to start a family. And it was good to tie his tribe to Brave Hawk's, especially now that Brave Hawk had made solid plans to bring his band of Chippewa to the big sky country to live as one with Night Wolf's people. When the two groups joined, doubled in their numbers, the hunt would also be doubled. They would be stronger against the whites, who were multiplying on the land of all red men much more quickly than Night Wolf even wanted to think about.

Yes, he had promised himself to another woman, who would be arriving soon for marriage. Yet his heart had just been taken by Marissa McHugh.

"You seem lost in thought," Joseph said. "Was it something I said?"

Night Wolf started, and smiled awkwardly. "My mind was with someone else," he admitted.

Joseph laughed. "A woman, no doubt." He reached for a journal and pored over its entries as Night Wolf turned his attention back to the jar of marbles.

"I have come today not only for myself but also for my mother and her friend, and my nephew," Night Wolf said. "My nephew, Little Moon, enjoys marbles. I would like several."

"Marbles it is," Joseph said. He took the jar from the shelf and unscrewed the lid, then pulled over a buckskin cloth and shook several of the marbles from the jar onto the cloth. "You choose. I shall place the ones you want in a bag."

Night Wolf saw Joseph take a small buckskin bag with a drawstring at the top from a stack of many more just like it.

With a forefinger he sorted through the marbles, choosing this one and that one until he had enough to fill the bag.

Joseph placed them in the bag, pulled the drawstring tight, then put the bag on top of the counter beside the other items Night Wolf had already gathered there—some musket balls and powder for his firearms, as well as two hatchets with tips painted the bright color of a red sunset. He had also chosen two blankets and some other, smaller items that would be placed in the parfleche bags that he had secured at the back of his horse.

"I would also like several pearl buttons for my mother and some red cloth," Night Wolf said, pointing to each as he mentioned it.

He smiled when he saw many pretty velveteen ribbons spread out along a shelf. They would be the perfect surprise gift for Shame on Face. He had seen such ribbons sewn onto her doeskin dresses and then tied into colorful bows.

He pointed to them. "And I would like several ribbons," he said. "I want some the color of the sky, the color of the sun and . . . those that are the color of the violets that live along the forest floor."

He could not resist buying something that was the same color as Marissa's eyes. Whenever Shame on Face wore a dress that displayed those ribbons on it, he would remember the very instant that he had looked into eyes of that same color.

"You are new to the land of big sky country,"

Night Wolf said as Joseph assembled the supplies. "Do you like it? Will you willingly stay for a good length of time?"

"I was here many years ago," Joseph said, smoothing the ribbons as he placed one and then another on the counter. "I was stationed at Fort Harris, but when my wife and I were to become parents of our beautiful daughter, Marissa, I preferred taking my family back to our home in Kansas. I was a major at that time. I resigned my post here, and when I arrived back in Kansas, I left the cavalry altogether to begin a life in trading. After my wife died, I needed to get away from the sorrowful memories. When I received word from my friend, Colonel Payton James, that he was stationed at Fort Harris, and wanted me to consider bringing my trading post here so that we could renew our friendship, I could not resist. I boarded a riverboat with my daughter and all of our belongings and supplies, and here we are. It is good to be back with my friend. We went to school together, we joined the cavalry together, we were stationed here at Fort Harris when we were both majors, and now we shall grow into old age together. And I look forward to a long and lasting relationship with you and your people."

"I hope for a long and lasting relationship with you as well," Night Wolf said.

He looked at all the items he had chosen today, then went out and got his pelts. He spread them out on the counter and watched as Trader Joe ran his hands slowly over their soft plushness. He saw a look of appreciation in Trader Joe's eyes. Night Wolf knew that he and this Trader Joe would have a fruitful relationship in the spring, and he looked forward to it.

After loading his supplies into the parfleche bags, Night Horse mounted and nodded farewell to Trader Joe, who stood at his door, smiling.

Night Wolf rode in a slow lope toward the mission to see if the young braves were still doing their assigned duties well enough. As he approached the potato patch, he saw Marissa again. He drew a tight rein and watched the lovely woman for a while, mostly from the back as she knelt on the ground, digging. With her long black hair hanging far down her back, she could have passed for an Indian. But when she seemed to feel his eyes on her, she turned to look at him, and he saw too well that she was anything but Indian. Her violet eyes, her pale skin, the dots of brown across her nose, which he had learned were called "freckles," proved her heritage.

As his eyes and Marissa's held, he felt a sensual stirring inside that no other woman had ever caused, yet he knew he had to fight his feelings. He could not forget that he had promised to marry his best friend's sister, Blue Star, and marrying Blue Star would strengthen the alliance between his Cree people and the Chippewa.

"Blue Star," he whispered.

Ay-uh, yes, he *must* keep repeating her name to keep her alive in his heart. Now it would be hard, for there was someone else to take her place.

The alliance! That was what he had to remember. That was the most important thing about all of this confusion that was now inside his very soul.

Chapter 4

The feel of someone watching her had caused Marissa to look up. She had almost known without looking that Night Wolf was behind her. He had had enough time to do his business at her father's trading post and was coming back for the young braves.

She was right.

He had stopped momentarily, but he was now riding toward the potato patch, his eyes still on her. Marissa felt a strange yet sweet feeling at the pit of her stomach.

When he came to the potato patch and dismounted close beside it, a feverish blush rushed to Marissa's cheeks, for he was still looking at her. Then he suddenly smiled and nodded at her.

That smile told her that he saw something special in her, as she did in him. It made her feel awkward, yet she returned the smile and nod, then resumed her digging. Night Wolf walked past her to Father Mulvaney, who was digging just behind her.

"I see that the young braves are still helping you," Night Wolf said. "That is good."

He smiled at the priest, then shifted his gaze to his braves, who stopped long enough to give him a nod of greeting.

Father Mulvaney slowly and painfully pushed himself up from the ground and stood beside Night Wolf. "You have an eager bunch of young braves," he said, looking approvingly from one youth to the next. Suddenly he winced and clutched his left side, smiling awkwardly at Night Wolf as he kneaded the pain out. "My age is catching up with me. One of these days I won't be able to do such labor as this.

"It is not so much the labor as it is getting up and down to do it," he amended and laughed. "I used to till a whole potato patch by myself without the first pain. Now look at me. I'm not worth much these days."

"Are there many more potatoes to be dug?" Night Wolf asked. As he spoke, he looked at the long rows that had not yet been upturned.

"Quite a few, but the children need not stay any longer," the priest said. "They have done enough. They can leave."

Night Wolf gazed at Father Mulvaney's bent

back and noted that the other priests were just as old and feeble. He could hear them groan sometimes as they moved from row to row to dig anew.

Then Night Wolf gave Marissa a sidewise glance. She, too, was still busy with her digging. She seemed to be purposely ignoring him now, though he knew by the way she had looked at him earlier that she was as taken by him as he was by her.

He looked at the elderly men at work, then at Father Mulvaney, and a plan came to him. Although he did see the need to help the older men, it was for another reason that he wanted to stay a while longer—a reason that he hoped would not be noticed.

Was not this an opportunity to be with, and talk to, the beautiful woman? He might never have such a chance again. He knew that he should not even want this time with her because of his promise to marry Blue Star, but he could not help himself.

"The braves will not leave until the work is *mee-gee-kee-shee-tako*, finished," he said. "Even I will help."

"You?" Father Mulvaney said, his eyes widening as Night Wolf eased his digging tool from his hand, then went to his knees and

made his way along the hills of dirt, laying potatoes aside as he dug them.

Father Mulvaney smiled to himself when he
saw how Marissa looked over her shoulder at
Night Wolf. The blush on her face was proof
positive of how the handsome Cree chief was
affecting her. He shifted his gaze to Night Wolf
and saw that he had hurried along his row
until he came side by side with Marissa. Father
Mulvaney saw how they stopped working
long enough to look into each other's eyes.

His smile turned into a frown, for he knew
the impossibilities of a relationship between a
white woman and a red man. It was something
that just didn't happen. If it did, the woman
would be shunned forever by the white community.

Although Father Mulvaney viewed such
prejudice as sinful, that was how it was, and
there was no way anyone could change such
biased opinions. Yet he knew no way to stop
what was happening between these two who
were so obviously attracted to one another.
Marissa was not Father Mulvaney's responsi-
bility. It would have to be her father who explained the situation to his one and only
daughter.

Father Mulvaney turned his gaze toward the
trading post and studied the windows. He was

glad that Joseph wasn't watching. Surely this attraction between his daughter and the powerful young chief would be only momentary. Then Night Wolf would return to his people and his daily activities with them, just as Marissa would return to her own usual activities.

Father Mulvaney's bones ached so much now that he wasn't sure he could even make it back to the mission. He welcomed Marissa and Night Wolf's assistance. With Night Wolf using the last digging tool, Father Mulvaney took an opportunity to rest. He ambled over to the shade of a tree and eased down to the ground, his pulse racing, his breathing ragged. He continued to watch Night Wolf and Marissa, his concern mounting as the two of them began talking as they dug and tossed one potato after another on the ground behind them.

"Oh, Night Wolf, *look*," Marissa said almost in a squeal, gesturing to a monarch butterfly as it fluttered directly in front of her face as though it were looking at her.

"Beauty attracts beauty," Night Wolf said, also watching the butterfly. "It is such a beautiful butterfly, as are you . . . *mee-kah-wah-diz-ee*, which in my language means 'beautiful.'"

Marissa felt the heat of a blush on her cheeks, for no man on this earth had ever paid her such a wonderful compliment—and this was not just any man, this was a handsome Cree chief, the man who had stolen her heart the very moment she had looked into his jet-black eyes.

"Thank you," she said shyly, yet she did not turn to Night Wolf. She didn't want to do anything to push the lovely creature away.

"Do you think that if I stretched my hand out toward the butterfly it might land on it, or would the movement frighten it?" she said, trying to keep her voice as low as possible, for the butterfly now fluttered even closer to her.

"Let us see what its plans are," Night Wolf said, watching the butterfly, which made a sharp turn and flew out of Marissa's sight, fluttered softly behind her, then began making its way around to the front of her again.

"Oh, it's gone," Marissa said. But just as she turned her head to follow the butterfly's flight, it was there again, and this time it landed on the tip of her nose.

She stood stone still so she would not frighten the butterfly away. But she could not help but giggle.

"Stay very, very still," Night Wolf said, enjoying these innocent moments with the woman he would have trouble putting out of his mind once he was away from her and involved in his chieftain duties again.

Blue Star. He kept repeating Blue Star's name to himself.

"But it tickles," Marissa whispered back to him as the butterfly moved slowly over her nose, its wings half stilled, its huge black eyes looking into hers.

"Let us see what else it might do before it leaves our lives *ah-pah-nay,* forever," Night Wolf said. He slowly eased his hand up, stopping when it was directly in front of Marissa's nose, so close that he was almost touching it. "Do not move. Just barely breathe . . ."

He moved his hand even closer and as he did, the butterfly crawled onto it. Night Wolf and Marissa watched the tiny creature amble around the palm of Night Wolf's hand, then suddenly take flight and flutter away, higher and higher until it was just a tiny fleck against the backdrop of blue sky.

"What a wonderful experience," Marissa said, sighing. "I shall never forget it."

"This is *penahque-geezis,* the moon of the falling leaves, the time of the year when monarchs from every corner of the land take their migration paths south, where they will remain until next spring. Then they will magically return to give pleasure to us who marvel over them," Night Wolf said. He resumed his digging, as did Marissa.

"Back home in Kansas, I saw monarch butterflies in the autumn," Marissa told him. "I had a lovely mimosa tree in my front yard, and its flowers attracted the butterflies. I shall always remember how the tree looked like a tree of butterflies as they clung to the mimosa blossoms in thick patches. Hummingbirds, too. Now that was a sight to see, especially when one of them would stop and perch to feed, for usually we see a hummingbird only in flight with its dizzying wings that are so beautiful to watch."

"You are a woman in love with nature," Night Wolf said, stopping to smile over at Marissa. "That is good. It is proof of your kind, sweet heart."

Marissa blushed again. She felt as though she had entered the portals of heaven.

Chapter 5

Joseph welcomed Major Bradley Coomer with a warm hug as the major came into his study, a room at the back of the trading post between the two bedrooms of the large cabin.

"It's nice of you to stop in for a visit," Joseph said. He admired how the young major looked so neat and well groomed in his blue uniform. He stood strong-backed. His jaw was square, his eyes blue, his hair worn neatly to his collar. He seemed always to be at attention, as though a colonel had just stepped into the room and it was expected of him. His only flaw was that damnable chip in his front tooth.

Afraid it might embarrass the young major, Joseph had not asked about it, but he would one day. It was something he just had to know.

Joseph gestured toward a chair. "Sit, young man," he said. "Let's talk."

"It is my pleasure, sir," Bradley said as he sat down on a plush leather chair opposite Joseph.

On one side of the room a roaring fire burned in a wide stone fireplace. On the opposite wall were windows looking out onto the huge yard that stretched to adjoin the land and gardens of the mission.

"As you know, Bradley, your colonel and I were best friends many years ago when we were both stationed here at Fort Harris, and even before then. We are from the same town in Kansas," Joseph said, remembering those days so long ago when the two majors aspired to become colonels.

His friend, Payton James, had succeeded. He was colonel and now happened to be stationed where they both had served as young men.

"Yes, I know of your association," Bradley said, idly running his long, lean fingers through his thick red hair. "I also know that you gave up your military career because of Marissa. That was valiant of you, to say the least."

"When my wife and I were blessed with a child, I saw it as more important to raise Marissa where it was civil than to raise her on land that was more savage than it is now," Joseph said, nodding.

"And then you chose to return," Bradley said, smoothing the front of his pristine blue uniform jacket, then resting his hands on his lap.

"I would never have returned here had my wife lived," Joseph said. "But when she died, I felt the need to be anywhere but Kansas, where my emotions were still raw over her passing. When I received a wire from Payton saying that he had been transferred to Fort Harris and that there was no trading post close to the Cree village, I grabbed the opportunity, and here I am. I have myself quite an establishment now, don't you think?"

"Yes, quite," Bradley said stiffly, his blue eyes level with Joseph's. "And I, for one, am very glad that you came to this area. Had you not, I would have never had the chance to meet Marissa."

"Then you are looking forward to the nuptials?" Joseph asked, his voice breaking. Even though he thought marriage was best for his daughter, he hated the idea that he was pushing her into the arms of someone who was still a stranger to them both.

But after seeing her take off too often alone on her horse, riding and exploring, not heeding the dangers of the area, he saw no other choice but to ensure that she was settled down into wifely duties.

"Very," Bradley said. "I appreciate how both

you and Colonel James chose me to court Marissa."

That word *court* made Joseph pause. He knew that this man was trying to court his daughter and that Marissa was fighting it.

And he understood why.

Although Payton had spoken highly of Bradley, saying that he was someone with a good future in the military, the kind of man any woman would be proud to call her husband, there was something about him that rankled with Joseph.

But Payton insisted that Bradley—his protégé no less—would make a fine husband and Marissa would have a comfortable life as a military wife, especially after Bradley became a colonel himself.

Joseph wondered if Bradley was so eager to marry Marissa only because he saw it as something his colonel wanted him to do, perhaps thinking that he had something to gain in the eyes of his superior officer.

But Joseph had to put that out of his mind. He knew that his daughter would be better off married. It would not only tame her wild side, it would stop any notion of hers to go and befriend the Cree, an idea that she had said she found exciting.

That was the final blow. He realized that he

had made the wrong decision to come to this land. His daughter becoming involved with an Indian in any capacity at all was the last thing he would want for his Marissa.

There were too many dangers in that.

"Sir, I came today to discuss the marriage and when it might take place," Bradley announced, having just come from Colonel James's office. The colonel had given his final blessing before Bradley even received it from Marissa's father. He felt himself one step closer to moving up in rank, for with someone like Colonel James looking out for his interests, how could he fail?

Yes, marrying the daughter of the colonel's best friend could only help push Bradley to the very top. That alone was his reason for marrying the woman. Otherwise, he would have preferred to remain single and have the perks of a single man. He enjoyed many a woman's company and didn't want to be saddled with only one.

But he was ready to do anything to advance himself in the military.

And he was not only advancing himself, he was getting one fine woman. She *was* beautiful. Who would not want to join such a woman in bed each night, even though he was used to choosing a different woman every time he had the need to have his sexual urges satisfied? At Fort Harris, there weren't any women close enough for him to have his pick.

"You do know that Marissa is the only reason the ceremony has not already been performed, do you not?" Joseph said. He leaned forward in his chair and peered more intently into the young major's eyes. "Do you find that, eh, offensive, that she is not all that ready to become your wife?"

Bradley shrugged. "I don't take it personally at all," he said smugly. "She is a young thing who just might not savor the thought of suddenly being tied down to the responsibilities of a wife. After we are married, she will see that it isn't all that bad."

"Then you can be patient for just a while longer, can't you?" Joseph asked. "I do not want to rush her into something she seems loath to do. But I do not want to wait much longer either."

"That word *loath* is harsh, don't you think?" Bradley said, easing up from the chair, idly walking over to a window to peer out. "If she . . . loathes . . . marriage, does not that mean that she . . . loathes . . . me?"

Joseph stood up and put a log on the grate of his fireplace, then turned his back to the warmth and stood with his hands clasped behind him. "I apologize for using such a word as that," he said. "It is only that Marissa has openly resented the matchmaking and has said that she is not ready to marry, that when she is, she wants to choose her own man."

"Then I see the importance of truly courting her," Bradley said. "I shall think on how it should be done, for I do want your daughter for my wife. There is something wild about her that has attracted me to her. And her long black hair makes her look as though she is part Indian." He laughed throatily. "I've always been attracted to Indian squaws." He looked quickly over his shoulder at Joseph, then gazed out the window again. "But I would never want one for a wife."

Joseph shuffled his feet nervously after hearing Bradley speak openly about his feelings toward Indian women.

There was no respect in the man's voice, which troubled Joseph, yet he had to get past his feelings and move ahead with the plans. It was imperative that he get his daughter married off—or that he returned to civilization in Kansas, where she could be single for as long as she wished.

There she had not faced danger head-on.

He did wish now that he had not uprooted everything and come to this wicked land, but he had. He had left his life in Kansas totally behind him.

Bradley turned his back to the window, pulled a toothpick from the front pocket of his uniform, and began picking at his teeth. Joseph thought the habit crude, but he dismissed it, since everything else about Bradley seemed decent.

Again Joseph noticed the ugly chip in one of Bradley's front teeth. This time he could not resist asking about it.

"Bradley, how'd you happen to chip your tooth?"

"I did it in a skirmish several years ago," Bradley said, flipping the toothpick into the fireplace.

"In a skirmish with an Indian?" Joseph asked, raising an eyebrow.

A gleam entered Bradley's eyes. He smiled. "Yep, and one I'll never forget," he said.

"Did the Indian die?" Joseph asked as Bradley went back to the window and stared out again.

Bradley laughed. "Let's say I earned my stripes," he said, giving Joseph a cold look over his shoulder.

That look made Joseph's heart go cold. He truly didn't know Bradley, nor what he was made of.

One thing that did seem certain was that the young major had a dislike for Indians—which might create such a problem that Joseph would have to change his mind about this man marrying his daughter.

Chapter 6

Joseph raised an eyebrow as Bradley continued to stand by the window. "What on earth are you finding so interesting at that window?" he asked, walking toward the young major.

"Something you might not want to see," Bradley said. "Yet on the other hand, you might find it mighty interesting."

Joseph sidled up next to Bradley and peered through the glass, his insides tensing when he did see what had held Bradley's attention for so long.

Not only did he see his daughter digging potatoes alongside the young Cree chief, but he also got to the window just in time to see Night Wolf brush some specks of dirt from Marissa's cheek.

It was a gesture that was much too intimate as far as he was concerned, and he felt himself go pale when he saw that Marissa did not push Night Wolf away.

It had been enough to see that the young chief had not gone on to his village, but had stopped at the large potato patch to help the priests dig potatoes, much less to see how interested he was in Marissa.

He then noticed the Cree braves who were also digging the rich soil and putting the potatoes in bags.

"What the hell is going on?" he said between clenched teeth. "What are those braves doing there? And what on earth is Marissa thinking, digging alongside them—especially Night Wolf? This is the last thing I'd expect to happen, and by God, this is the last time it will. I'm going to get my daughter away from those Indians."

As he started to leave the room, he heard Bradley chuckle behind him.

He narrowed his eyes angrily at the young major. "What in damnation are you finding so funny about this?" he growled. "That's the woman you plan to marry, and you think it's laughable that she has made acquaintance with Indians?"

"You should've known that when you brought your daughter to Injun country she'd have an encounter or two with them," Bradley said, smirking. Then he gave Joseph a dark frown. "And, yes, if you want me to have anything to do with your daughter, especially marry her, you'd best make sure no Injun does anything more than wipe dirt from her face. I wouldn't lay a hand on her myself, if I knew that any more than that had happened."

Joseph was startled by such vehemence in this young man. The more he knew about him, the less likable he became.

Yet there it was, out there in the potato patch, exactly why he had to look past the major's shortcomings and make certain his daughter was married off to him soon.

He could imagine the stardust in his daughter's eyes when she looked at Night Wolf. He was a handsome man and surely intriguing as hell to Marissa.

Because of her past, oh, Lord, he *had* to get her away from Night Wolf. He couldn't afford for her to get too involved with any of the Indians in this area.

He had thought that the past was just that— past—and that there would be no way that the truth could be revealed. But now? He knew that he had been wrong to think it would never catch up with them.

He should've stayed in Kansas!

He turned quickly on his heel and ran through the trading post, then outside. He waved his hands in the air as he called Marissa's name.

Everyone stopped their digging and stared at him. Even his daughter, who was now standing, had a perplexed look on her face. He realized that he had gone about this in the wrong way.

Damn it all to hell, the fuss he was making was only bringing more attention to the problem at hand. Even with the knowledge that what he was doing was beyond what a normal father would do about a daughter associating with Indians, Joseph continued running toward Marissa, waving his arms.

"Marissa, come home this instant!" he shouted. "Get away from those Indians!"

Marissa was stunned into numbness by her father's crude, strange behavior.

Or had he seen how taken she was with Night Wolf?

She questioned why her father had, through the years, warned her about getting too friendly with Indians. He had uprooted everything he owned in Kansas and had come to this beautiful country to establish a trading post, which was built mainly to have trade *with* Indians.

On the journey west all he talked about was the rich, beautiful pelts that would be brought to his trading post, which he would then ship to various parts of the country for more money than he could ever imagine making in Kansas.

He had also been eager to be with his friend Payton again after growing up together and joining the cavalry "to see the world," he had laughingly told her. That world had mainly been this very land, where he had been stationed as a young major.

Her father had fallen in love with the land and had left it only because of Marissa, who he said needed a normal home with normal schooling.

That was what he had told her, yet she had always wondered if there was something more behind his having moved to Kansas so quickly after Marissa was conceived.

Once they returned to this land, surely he had known that he could not keep her from involvements with Indians. He had to know that she would be around them, for she was not the sort to hide at the back of the trading post when they were making their trades.

It was exciting. As she had found it exciting to have made an instant friend in Night Wolf.

She couldn't understand why her father was reacting this way. He himself had met the young chief and knew what sort of man he was.

Night Wolf had more gentle traits than many men that she had known through the years, especially Bradley, the man her father had chosen for her to marry. Bradley was crude to the point of being disgusting. He had tried to corner her when her father wasn't looking, to sneak a kiss, and even to feel her breasts.

And she was puzzled as to why her father was rushing her into this marriage with such a cad.

Since their arrival, her father had changed. He seemed to be on guard at all times whenever she was anywhere but in their living quarters of the trading post or with the priests at the mission.

When Joseph reached her and stood glowering at her with hands on his hips, Marissa knew that she had no choice but to go with him. She gave Night Wolf a look of apology, excused herself, then went to the trading post with her father.

As soon as they got inside and he had slammed the door behind them, he started in on her, so harshly that she felt trapped. Worse than that, she felt heartsick, for she knew that Night Wolf had to have been insulted by her father's rude behavior. She wanted to rush back outside and tell him that her father didn't mean the insults, that he was just not himself today, that normally he was a genteel man whose heart was as big as the western sky.

But her father pulled her aside, away from the door, then stood with his back to it in case she tried to flee his wrath.

She stood stiffly, her eyes slowly taking on a challenging look. She had never been as embarrassed by her father as she had been today. He was becoming someone she didn't know. If her mother had been alive, even she would have seen the change in him. Her mother wouldn't have liked this change. Nor did Marissa.

"Marissa, haven't I warned you about Indians?" Joseph said, his hands in fists at his sides. "Haven't I told you to be wary of redskins, to stay away from them? Didn't you see how that young chief was openly showing affection for you? Surely he sees you as wife material. Marissa, the thought sickens me. *Sickens* me."

Marissa was aghast. She couldn't see how anyone could be sickened by Night Wolf.

"Father, how can you say such things?" she blurted out. "Night Wolf is nice, kind, and he would never harm me. And as far as him seeing me as 'wife material,' as you so crudely call it, I doubt that. I'm sure there are countless beautiful Indian women for him to choose from for a wife."

She paused, then took a step closer to him. "And Father, what is this thing about Indians that you would embarrass me in front of not only Night Wolf but also the young braves? Father, you came here to trade with Indians. Do you think your behavior today will gain you any points with them? Why would they come and trade here at your trading post if you look to them as—as—savages."

"I never called anyone a savage," Joseph said, his voice drawn. "And if what I did today causes ill feelings, so be it. I'm concerned with only one thing at this moment. *You*."

He started to touch her cheek gently, then flinched when he saw her step back out of reach.

"Marissa, go to your room," he ordered. "And listen to me when I tell you that I forbid you ever to go near that Indian chief again. Do you hear? Forbid!"

Marissa was stunned that he could use that word *forbid*. Knowing the worst of what he meant by saying it—that she couldn't see Night Wolf again, much less talk with him— made her heart skip a beat. She knew her father well enough to know that when he was this angry about something, there was hardly anything anyone could do to change his mind.

She knew that at this moment she had no choice but to do as he said.

Sulking, she rushed from him and hurried to her room. She slammed the door closed without ever noticing Bradley at the door of the study, witnessing everything.

Joseph went to Bradley, grabbed him by an arm, and took him into the privacy of the study, kicking the door closed behind them.

He turned to face Bradley. "I want to settle this marrying thing once and for all," he stormed, his fists on his hips. "But before we can finalize things between us, Bradley, I feel I owe you the full truth about Marissa."

Bradley's eyes narrowed. "*What* truth?" he asked warily.

Chapter 7

Still stunned by Trader Joe's treatment of his daughter, which in a sense was also against Night Wolf himself, Night Wolf stood staring at the trading post. Earlier Trader Joe had not seemed to be a man of prejudice. He had even seemed eager to be friends.

But that was before his daughter showed kindness toward Night Wolf—an Indian.

When he felt a hand on his arm, Night Wolf turned and found Father Mulvaney standing at his side, an apology in the depths of his faded gray eyes.

"I am sorry for Joseph's insensitivity toward you while scolding his daughter," Father Mulvaney said sadly. "I have known this man for only one month, but during that time I have found him to be likable and kindhearted. And he uprooted himself from his life in Kansas to come here and establish a trading post that will benefit you and your people."

"It is not for you to apologize for the crudeness of another *chee-mo-ko-man*," Night Wolf said as Father Mulvaney eased his hand from his arm. "But I will accept it anyway with a friendly heart."

"That is because your heart is filled with goodness," Father Mulvaney said. "You would be the sort to look past such prejudice. I imagine you have come face-to-face with it all of your life. The world could be a much happier place if everyone accepted each other as they were born, no matter the color of the skin or the customs they practice. It could be such a place of peace, a heaven on earth."

Night Wolf knew that Father Mulvaney lived in a dreamworld of how he wished things could be, when life was anything but what his dreams brought to him. It had taken Joseph's harsh words and behavior today to awaken Night Wolf all over again to the prejudices against people of his skin color.

Then again, how could he ever forget those moments with Marissa? *Her* skin was white, yet she was so openly sweet and friendly. Her eyes spoke to him. He knew that she had yearnings within her, just as he had inside himself. She needed a man, just as he needed a woman.

But after seeing how her father felt about her

having any sort of relationship with people of Night Wolf's skin color, he realized the impossibility of the two of them ever satisfying those longings.

"It is time to get my braves to their homes," he said, trying hard to push Marissa from his mind.

"Yes, I understand," Father Mulvaney said as he watched the braves work. Only a few potatoes remained in the ground. "The boys have most certainly worked off their debt."

Night Wolf saw the many bags that lay along the ground, overflowing with potatoes. He smiled with approval at one young brave and then at another as they noticed him standing there, watching.

"I have a surprise for you all," Father Mulvaney said. "I shall count off seven bags of potatoes. They are for you to take home with you for your people. Please take them with my blessing."

Night Wolf was amazed that Father Mulvaney could be this generous and forgiving, but he knew how much his people would enjoy the potatoes, so he nodded and smiled his acceptance.

"*Mee-gway-chee-wahn-dum*, thank you, for your kindness," he said. "The women of my village thank you. They always enjoy your gifts."

He placed a hand on each of the young braves' shoulders. *"Mee-gee-kee-shee-tako*, it is finished here. Your debt to Father Mulvaney has been paid," he said softly. "Take the bags of potatoes that the priest has been so generous to give our people and put them on the backs of your ponies. We will be going home now."

Father Mulvaney and Night Wolf watched until the bags were secured and the young braves were mounted and ready to travel, then Father Mulvaney walked Night Wolf to his own horse.

Night Wolf swung into the saddle, lifted his reins, and gave the priest another warm smile of thanks.

"I again apologize for Trader Joe's rudeness," Father Mulvaney said, squinting as the sinking sun in the west shone in his old eyes. "It might have been because he felt threatened—he might have seen you showing too much attention to his daughter, as though you might have an interest in her for a wife."

Night Wolf's eyes widened. It did seem, even to the priest, that the reason for Trader Joe's anger was Night Wolf's attentiveness to his daughter. He would never forget the harshness of Trader Joe's words, or the anger and resentment in his eyes as he took Marissa away to the trading post.

"His anger was wasted, then. The white man has nothing to fear from me, for I have chosen my future bride," Night Wolf said, even though he wished that what he admitted was not so. He did not want to marry Blue Star. "It was just a friendly conversation between myself and the white woman, nothing more."

"I see," Father Mulvaney said, hearing words that he found hard to believe, for he had seen the look in Night Wolf's eyes as he had talked with Marissa.

He heard how she had giggled when Night Wolf coaxed the butterfly off her nose onto his hand. So much had been said between them when they had gazed into one another's eyes. There was no doubt that each had been attracted to the other.

"I will be getting married soon," Night Wolf said, still feeling the need to make the priest understand. "Blue Star, the woman with whom I have made plans for marriage, is of the St. Croix band of Chippewa and should be arriving soon. She is the sister of a chief who is a friend from my past. She understands the role of a chief's wife. She will be good for me."

"Blue Star," Father Mulvaney said, nodding. He knew that Night Wolf was not being altogether honest with him, and that when he had spoken the name of Blue Star, it had not been with vigor or love. It was mentioned out of duty.

However, when Night Wolf spoke Marissa's name, a certain light came into his eyes, and a smile crossed his lips, proving to Father Mulvaney that this young chief *was* attracted to Marissa but was fighting his feelings. After all, he was duty-bound to another woman—a woman he did not love.

"Thank you again, my friend, for your understanding," Night Wolf said, smiling down at Father Mulvaney. "And there will be much delight taken when the cooked potatoes are served to the people of my village. Thank you and farewell."

"You are quite welcome," Father Mulvaney said. "It was my pleasure to help in some small way to feed your people."

Night Wolf smiled at Father Mulvaney again, then flicked his reins and rode off with his braves following closely behind on their ponies.

He could not help but look toward the trading post as he approached it before making a wide turn to the left, which would take him to his village.

No matter what Father Mulvaney said, or

how many apologies were made for the trader's evil tongue and hateful ways, Night Wolf could not understand a father who could treat such a gentle, sweet daughter so cruelly, or a man who could be so kind to Night Wolf one instant and then in the next act as though Night Wolf was too dirty to be near his child.

Night Wolf knew now that he could never like the man. He would trade with him, but nothing more. His thoughts returned to Blue Star. He had promised to marry her, but could he?

The white woman was in his heart. She was in his blood. She was in his very soul.

His heart skipped a beat when he saw Marissa standing at a window at the back of the trading post cabin. He concluded that it was her bedroom. Their eyes met and held. In her eyes he could see a mixture of anger and hurt. Night Wolf understood where these feelings came from. She was angry over what her father had done.

Before riding on past the trading post, he slowed his horse to a trot and gazed at Marissa for a moment longer. It was hard not to linger. Everything about her awakened so much in him that had lain dormant. He had finally met a woman that made him feel fire inside his heart.

Yet he must do what was right for his people.

An alliance with the Chippewa had been planned, and marrying Blue Star would ensure it. He must make certain that nothing caused that alliance to fail. There was strength in numbers. With his people coming together as one with the St. Croix band of Chippewa, the numbers needed to ward off possible attacks from whites were there.

He expected the arrival of the entire St. Croix band of Chippewa soon, and with them Blue Star. He had not seen her since she was five.

Torn over how he felt, he was not sure now what he could do about things that had changed in a heartbeat today.

How could he forget this woman, this white woman, Marissa, whose very voice awakened everything sensual within him?

He knew that he could not forget her. No matter what transpired when his friend Brave Hawk arrived with his sister and his entire band of Chippewa, Night Wolf would not be able to let go of feelings that ran like wildfire through him every time he saw Marissa in his mind's eye. No matter how Marissa's father tried to stand in the way, he could not give up something that had come so quickly and wonderfully to his heart.

He took one long last look at Marissa, the woman that he longed to cherish.

Now that he knew which room was hers, he would come to her in the dark.

He *must* talk with her, to sort through his feelings.

But then how could he explain to her about Blue Star?

And if he did decide to give his all to the white woman, how could he explain to a best friend that he could not marry his sister, that his heart belonged to another?

The alliance.

Would the St. Croix band of Chippewa turn away from Night Wolf and his people and return to the Minnesota Territory if Night Wolf refused to marry Blue Star?

He gave Marissa a soft smile, his spirit soaring when she returned one of her own. Then he rode onward, his heart heavy, for how could he have found someone he had loved instantly, only to lose her?

He had much to work out in his heart and mind.

Chapter 8

Still not able to understand how her father could be so demanding of her after having been so kind and understanding throughout her life, Marissa could not get past her resentment.

And then there was that moment when Night Wolf had caught her standing at the window. The way he returned her gaze made her heart warm even now. There had been sparks all over again.

Yet her father seemed determined to keep them apart.

She knew that he was looking out for her welfare, but still it didn't make sense that he would be this adamant about her not being around Indians, especially since they had come west with the sole purpose of trading with them.

Had her father intended to keep her locked away during trading season? Was that how he had planned to deal with the possibility of her coming face-to-face with Indians?

"Why, Father?" she whispered.

Why would he be this concerned about her talking with the Cree chief? Never had she met such a gentle-speaking man as Night Wolf. She had enjoyed those moments with him as they dug together. And then there was the butterfly.

"I shall never forget . . ."

No, she would never forget how that butterfly had caused sweetness between her and Night Wolf. Or how Night Wolf had smiled at her before he rode off to return to his home and people. Those sorts of moments were something dreams were made of—moments frozen in time. Precious moments like those would get her through these next few hours when she would be trying to understand her irrational father.

Sighing, she lit a kerosene lamp and sat down in the plushly cushioned chair beside her reading table. The lamp shone softly upon a book chosen from the many that she had brought along from her family library back in Kansas City. She loved to read and write poetry.

But tonight she found it hard to concentrate on anything but Night Wolf—and her anger toward her father.

Determined to get past these tumultuous feelings and her confusion about her father, Marissa opened the novel at the satin ribbon marker she had placed in it and tried to resume where she had left off earlier that morning before breakfast. The story was about a handsome knight who was pursuing his golden-haired love in a huge, airy castle in England, and how the beautiful woman's father was ready to kill the knight to keep him away from his daughter.

"Oh, this will not do," Marissa said aloud, slamming the book shut. The story was too much like her own, except that her father surely wouldn't kill Night Wolf to keep him away from Marissa.

"No, he wouldn't—would he?" she whispered to herself, her heart skipping a beat. As angry as her father was over her chance meeting and those brief moments with Night Wolf, might he really be capable of doing anything necessary to keep them apart?

"This just won't do," she muttered, realizing how daft she would seem to someone who saw her actually arguing with herself out loud.

She suddenly felt like anyone *but* herself. Having been with Night Wolf, having fallen for the handsome chief, had changed her.

She would never be the person she had been

before she looked into his mystical dark eyes and heard his mesmerizing voice.

She was a woman in love, and she had to find a way to make certain she could be with Night Wolf again to test the reality of his feelings for her.

Tears pooled in her eyes as she thought of her precious mother. She missed her mother so much at this moment. Her mother had been her confidante. She could talk with her about anything. It would have been wonderful to share her feelings about Night Wolf with her. Marissa knew that her mother would not have made the same demands of her that her father had made.

Her mother would have understood her feelings. She would have been able to talk with her about them without fearing a lecture against Night Wolf when she was through.

"Mother, how I do miss you," she whispered, wiping tears from her eyes.

She gazed at the closed door. She knew what she must do. Her father was now her only confidant, and needing to make him see reason, she had no choice but to go to him.

She must make him tell her why he had treated her and the chief so unjustly today. She would not leave his sight until he explained himself.

"Yes, I must," she said, jumping to her feet.

She *would* discover why he had treated her so badly in front of the others. Their puzzlement over his actions had been reflected in their eyes. It could only point to him being a prejudiced person, and she had never known that side of him. She hoped that she was wrong, and that he had a vastly different reason—a reason that might make some sense to her.

She hurried from her room to the store at the front of the cabin. When she didn't find her father there, she went to the front door and looked outside for him. But he wasn't there either, so she left the large outer room. She walked down the corridor, then stopped and frowned as she heard his voice behind the closed door of his study.

Bradley Coomer was there speaking of marriage to her father again, and possibly even setting a date, a date she would never accept, for she would *not* marry him.

There was only one man on this earth that she would consider marrying, and that man was forbidden to her.

Her father had never forbidden her anything. That he had done so now still did not make any sense.

If her father had had a terrible encounter

with Indians in his past, she would understand. But he hadn't. Even when he had been in the cavalry, he had not gone against Indians in fierce battles. He had been in this area, where the Cree were the main tribe, a tribe who had not fought against whites.

She started to knock on the door, then stopped. What was being said inside the room made her go cold.

She stiffened as she heard her father tell Bradley that he must know her true heritage before he married her. He feared that if Marissa had a baby, and it came out to look Indian, then Bradley would know that his wife was part Indian herself.

Marissa felt faint as her father told his story. Years ago, when he was at Fort Harris, he went horseback riding alone. Halfway between the fort and the Cree village, he found a newborn baby wrapped in an Indian blanket.

Her father went on to say that he determined the baby had been born to an Indian mother because she had black hair and wore a string of beads around her neck. He knew that no white woman would place an Indian necklace on a child. He had concluded that the child had a white father, surely from a love affair, and that her mother's people wouldn't allow her to keep the child. It was a custom of Indians to abandon a baby if the mother or father did not want to claim it as theirs for a particular reason.

Joseph said that his wife had wanted a child, but was unable to become pregnant. He told no one about finding the baby, not even his best friend, Payton James. To keep it a secret from the soldiers at the fort, he immediately resigned his post, and the family soon left for their home in Kansas.

Only his wife and he knew that the baby was not theirs by birth. Nevertheless, they had raised Marissa with all of their love, so proud of her that they had never thought back again about how they came to have her.

And now someone else knew.

Bradley.

Again Joseph said that he had confided in Bradley only because it would not be fair to him if he didn't know. One day he might discover the truth when a child was born to him and Marissa.

Joseph hoped that this didn't make any difference. Chances were, if they had a child, it would be white, for surely there was more white in Marissa than red; except for her black hair, she didn't look Indian.

When they moved back west he had not even considered that someone might discover

Marissa's heritage. He didn't think there would ever be a way for anyone to discover who she truly was. But he did think that it was only fair that the man she would marry should know her true blood kin. He pleaded with Bradley not to tell anyone else. The Indian mother could still be somewhere close, possibly even at the Cree village. He would never want the Indians to know that Marissa was kin to any of them.

With tears flowing from her eyes, and torn with so many feelings—mainly of having lived a lie all of her life—Marissa listened to her father ask Bradley if knowing this about her made a difference?

There was an obvious pause—Bradley didn't answer Joseph right away. Joseph reminded him once again that Marissa was more white than red and that surely the baby would be the same.

And he recalled Bradley's having said earlier that Indian squaws intrigued him.

Marissa was aware of the stony silence in her father's study as he awaited Bradley's reply.

She wished that she could be there to see the look in the major's eyes.

Surely he saw his chance at making points

with the colonel dashed. He could not possibly want to marry Marissa now.

She had figured out something about Bradley that her father had not discovered yet, or did not want to admit to: Bradley was more interested in getting a boost in the cavalry by marrying the daughter of the colonel's best friend than in wanting Marissa because he had any sort of love for her.

She held her breath as she waited for him to speak his mind.

Bradley was stunned. He had the blessing of Colonel James to marry Marissa soon. Marrying her could have helped Bradley in his career, but he could not envision ever being married to a "breed"—a woman who was part Indian and part white.

He was from St. Louis. He had seen many breed women working in the dance halls and saloons, and he knew how men jeered at them and poked fun at them, calling them savage squaws. He could not take the chance of being laughed at for marrying the same sort of woman. He wanted to go far in the military, but not with a breed as a wife.

"I said that squaws intrigue me, but I also said that I'd never want to marry one, especially not a breed," Bradley said. He remembered how he had thought that he would do anything to get a position as colonel, but now he knew that he wouldn't. He would not marry a halfbreed! He must chance losing Colonel James's respect and help.

"No, Joseph, I won't marry Marissa," he said coldly. "Knowing what I know about her now, she would be the last woman on this earth that I would marry."

Shocked by all that she had heard and by what Bradley had just said, Marissa felt rooted to the spot.

She couldn't move even when Bradley rushed out of the room and slammed into her, the impact knocking her to the floor.

She lay there, her teary eyes looking up at Bradley, whose own eyes were cold as he glared down at her.

She turned away and did not look up again until the slamming of the front door gave proof of Bradley's quick exit.

Then she heard other footsteps. She stiffened, then turned slowly and looked up at her father.

When he saw her there, his face paled and he took an unsteady step away from her.

"You . . . heard . . . it all?" he gasped out.

"Every word," Marissa said, a sob lodging in her throat as she pushed herself up from the floor. "Father, why didn't you tell me the truth?

My whole life has been a lie. I have an Indian mother?"

"You do, and you also have a white father. Why else would your skin be white?" he said, reaching out for her, flinching when she stepped away from him. "Marissa, I couldn't let anyone know the truth about you. The white community would have shunned you. You saw Bradley's reaction. Everyone would have reacted in the same way. Your life would have been ruined. Haven't you been happy?"

"Yes, but now? You told the worst person of all about me," Marissa said between sobs. "You told Bradley. Did you see the contempt in his eyes? I saw it when he looked down at me. It gives me chills even now."

"Bradley knows, but it was only right that I told him. He was going to be your husband," Joseph said, nervously clasping and unclasping his hands.

"Did you ever consider asking me if I would truly marry such a man?" Marissa said, her voice catching. "You knew that I didn't like him. I had not intended to marry him. And now you've told him a secret that you protected so well? Father, you should have talked to me first, to seek my true feelings about this marriage. None of this would have ever had to be revealed. Not even I would have had to know. Now that I do? I'm so torn."

"I'm sorry, baby," Joseph said, again reaching out for her, but she still denied him. "I just expected that you would eventually care enough for him to marry him. He has such a good future ahead of him. He could have made life so comfortable for you."

"You would have wanted me married to someone I loathe, only because—" she began, but he interrupted her.

"Only because I wanted to protect you," he said. "And it was only right that Bradley should know the truth about you. I believed that he was going to be your husband. But now he sees you as a redskin, a breed. That's the very reason I never told anyone, and I wish now that I hadn't told him. I know how stupid it was of me to bring you back here to the very place where you were born."

"Where I was born, and not to the woman I thought was my mother," Marissa said, then burst into tears and ran from her father. She dashed outside, saddled and mounted her horse.

Joseph watched from the door as Marissa rode away.

He wanted to stop her, but knew she needed to work off her frustrations alone. He would talk to her again when she returned. He could not believe that this had happened, but he should have known when he brought her back here that it might.

He should have known.

He had only himself to blame for what happened now.

Chapter 9

Colonel Payton James was taking a stroll outside of the fort's walls. He stopped suddenly when he heard the approach of a horse. He turned and saw Marissa riding off, tears streaming down her lovely face. He looked to the trading post and saw Joseph standing there alone. He wondered what might have happened between them. He knew that Joseph would not want her to leave unescorted. Payton knew how protective Joseph was of his daughter.

Joseph had complained to Payton about Marissa sneaking off. Now Joseph knew that she was leaving but he was not going after her? It didn't make any sense.

Payton wanted to ask what had happened, but he knew that such a question might overstep the boundaries of their friendship.

He turned back to Marissa, her black hair flying in the wind. So much about Marissa—

especially her hair—reminded him of a love from long ago. A woman he could not marry because he had chosen the military life. He had finally asked to be reassigned to a post away from Fort Harris.

He had only recently returned to this fort and he felt uncertain about what to do. When he had left this area, he had left behind many memories. He had left a woman he would always love, but he had turned his back on her.

He had vivid memories of holding her hand as they walked in the moonlight, and of making passionate love with her beneath the stars.

He wanted to search for her, yet he knew better than to try to find out if she was still in the area. If he saw her again, even as an older woman, he would want her, need her, again. And she would surely spit at his feet because he had turned his back on their love.

She had been ready to leave her world for his. Instead, he had chosen his career over a lasting love, and never married anyone. His career was his life. A life that was so lonesome at times, it tore at his very being. Too often he was tempted to search for his one and only love. It would be a miracle if he could hold her again, tell her how much he had always loved her. He ached to apologize for having abandoned her.

He wondered if she was still with her husband, or if she had left him.

In time, he would look for her. The need to see her again chipped away at his heart as each day passed, especially since she might still be living close to the fort.

"Soft Voice," he whispered. He closed his eyes and saw her in his mind's eye as she was those many years ago, when she was young and vibrant, and so beautiful she had taken his breath away.

Chapter 10

Little Moon's excited squeals brought Night Wolf from his thoughts of Marissa and her father's treatment of her, and his insults to Night Wolf.

On one side of his heart he held wonderful memories of the white woman and the moments he had spent with her in the potato patch. On the other side he held resentment for Trader Joe. He was not sure what to do about both emotions.

He had never expected to fall in love so quickly, but since he had, he knew he must come to terms with his feelings and decide how to act on them.

"Uncle Night Wolf, I have never seen such pretty marbles as these," Little Moon said as he shook the marbles out of the small buckskin bag onto the floor mat in the bright light of the fire. "And this time you have brought so many to me. I have enough to share with my friends."

Little Moon gave Night Wolf a pleading look. "Do you care if I give some of these to my closest friends?" he asked. "They are not as fortunate as I am. They do not have such a generous uncle." He smiled, his dark eyes dancing. "I am the most fortunate of all children my age in our village. Not only do I have an uncle who cares deeply for me but he is also our people's proud chief!"

Night Wolf chuckled and patted Little Moon on his head. Night Wolf's sister, Moon Song, paused from sewing a new pair of moccasins, her eyes filled with adoration when she looked at Little Moon.

"Nephew, those kind words are appreciated tonight more than you will ever know," Night Wolf said. "*Mee-gway-chee-wahn-dum*, thank you. And, yes, you can share the marbles with your friends. It proves your kind heart. Kindness will get you more in life than being stingy and bitter."

"My brother, I sense that something did not go well at the trading post," Moon Song said. "Do you wish to talk about what happened? Or is it something that you must sort out yourself?"

"I will speak of it to you soon," Night Wolf

said, watching Little Moon as he gathered the marbles, then scooped them into the bag. "Let Little Moon go on with what he is doing. This is his time. Not mine."

"I want to go now and show my friends my marbles, and then let them choose which ones they want for themselves," Little Moon said, tying the bag closed as he rose to his feet. He raced to the entrance flap and shoved it aside, then stopped and turned to Night Wolf. "Again, thank you, Uncle. I love you."

"As I love you," Night Wolf said. "Go. Enjoy your friends. I will stay a while with your mother."

Little Moon hurried out.

Night Wolf sat down beside Moon Song, his eyes on the fire, lost in thought about what had happened that day. Whenever he thought of the white woman, he felt a warm glow inside his heart.

How could he ignore such feelings? He knew that he could not.

"What happened today that makes such a look in your eyes?" Moon Song asked, reaching over to place a hand on Night Wolf's arm. "My brother, did the owner of the trading post cause you these feelings? Is he not a good man, one who will deal fairly with our people after the rich spring hunt?"

"At first I saw him as a fair man, and then—" Night Wolf paused.

"And then?" his sister asked. "What happened, brother? Tell me why your mood now is so quiet, so solemn. Is it only because of something that happened between you and the trader? Or is it also because our young braves stole from the priests?"

"A part of it is because of Trader Joe, but at this moment none of it is because of the young braves," Night Wolf said. Then he gave his sister a pensive look and said, "It is because of an *ee-quay*, Moon Song."

"A woman?" Moon Song asked, raising her eyebrows. "My brother, what woman could you be talking about? No *ee-quay* is at the mission."

Then she leaned forward. "You are speaking of a woman you saw at the trading post?"

"Not at the trading post, but with the priests in the potato patch," Night Wolf said, again seeing Marissa's eyes when the butterfly landed on her nose. In his heart he still heard her sweet laughter.

"Was her skin the color of ours, or . . . was it white?" Moon Song asked guardedly.

"Her skin is as pale and as soft as the petals of a white mountain lily," he said. He looked away as he realized just how that might have sounded to his sister.

"You met a woman who has quickly intrigued you?" Moon Song asked. "A white woman?"

"She was treated rudely by her *gee-ba-ba*, father, today in my presence, and the braves as well as the priests were also there," Night Wolf said. "Her father's anger was stirred by our talking and laughing as we dug potatoes for the priests."

"Then the anger was more because of you, not his daughter?" Moon Song asked. "Because you were with her, enjoying her company, the man showed his prejudice against you?"

Night Wolf nodded. "She is a kindhearted woman, someone I know that you would enjoy, because you are of the same fabric as she," he said. "I feel sad for her having to live with such a man, who shows one side of his nature one minute, the other the next. His ugly side is what embitters me. He should not have shown such animosity toward his daughter associating with me, especially in the presence of our young braves."

"Then you are more concerned about how this prejudice will affect our braves than anything else?" Moon Song asked, searching his eyes.

"That, as well as that my heart has been stolen today by this woman whose father shows such resentment toward me," Night Wolf said. He gazed deeply into his sister's eyes. "But how can I follow my heart? I promised to marry Blue Star to create a strong alliance with the Chippewa. Now I am torn between duty to our people and love for Marissa."

"Oh, my brother, I can feel how torn you are," Moon Song said, trying to hide her shock over knowing how a white woman had affected her chieftain brother. He had never spoken like this of any woman before.

It was obvious that his feelings were true, and Moon Song understood his dilemma. Blue Star and Brave Hawk might even arrive tonight. What then would her brother do with these feelings that were tearing him apart?

How could he have fallen in love so quickly, and with a white woman?

She lowered her eyes as she recalled just how quickly she had fallen in love with her husband and how she ached even now for him. He had died so young and so needlessly. He had been ambushed by renegades while he was on his way home from a hunt. Life could be so cruel, so complicated.

"You do not condemn me, then, for having

feelings for a woman of a different color than ours?" Night Wolf asked softly. "That I have even allowed it to happen?"

"I would never condemn you for anything. I know that everything you do is from your heart and with much thought and consideration of others," Moon Song said. She got to her knees and twined her arms around his neck. "I wish I could help you, but it is something that you alone must figure out and deal with."

He hugged her as well. "One minute I lean toward my duty to our people, and the next, I lean toward allowing my heart to lead me to my decision. That path always leads to the white woman," he said.

She eased away from him and looked into his eyes. "I have loved and followed my heart," she murmured. "But you have more to think about when you make your final decision. I am not a leader. You are always wise in your choices. So shall you be now."

The laughter of many young braves wafted into the tepee, reminding Night Wolf of the joy in his nephew's eyes brought by the gift of marbles. His mother and Shame on Face enjoyed all that he had taken to them when he returned from the trading post. It gave Night Wolf joy to give joy.

"Let us see what the braves think of Little

Moon's marbles," he said, rising. He held out a hand for his sister. "Come."

Moon Song laughed softly, took his hand, then went out of the tepee with him, stopping outside when they found Little Moon and a circle of his friends.

Little Moon had emptied his bag of the marbles and had spread them in a wide circle for his ten best friends to see.

"Choose one each," he told them, proud to have something that he could share with so many. "Did not my uncle, your chief, choose the most beautiful marbles that one could ever want to have?"

"You are generous," Eagle Wing said, already reaching for one. He held it up between his fingers to the glow of the huge outdoor fire. "See the colors of the rainbow in this one? I would choose this one if you are willing to part with it, Little Moon."

"It is yours," Little Moon said, proudly puffing out his chest. Then he turned toward another young brave. "Small Fox, which do you like?"

Small Fox reached for one that was streaked with cream and orange colors. He plucked it up and held it out for all to see. "This one," he said, beaming.

This went on until each of the ten children had a marble.

Night Wolf marveled over his nephew's kind heart. He had the beginnings of a proud, generous leader, who one day might walk in his uncle's footsteps as chief unless Night Wolf brought a son into this world.

A son, he thought.

He did want children. Many of them. But first he had to take a wife. Again his thoughts strayed to Marissa. No matter how much he wrestled with his feelings and his sense of duty to his people, he could not get past his need of this white woman.

He knew that the alliance between his people and the St. Croix band of Chippewa was already strong. Why else would they be traveling all the way from the land of lakes to join the Wolf band of Cree? But if their chief became angered over his sister being hurt by the Cree chief, could everything change? Or was Brave Hawk a good enough friend to understand that a man's heart led him to a particular woman, whether it was Blue Star or Marissa?

Surely Brave Hawk would want Night Wolf to marry the woman he loved, for would not Night Wolf want the same for his friend if he finally found a woman with whom he wished to share his life?

"My brother, I think you need to be alone," Moon Song said, just loud enough for Night Wolf to hear. "You need to sort things out inside your heart so that the troubled look in your eyes will go away. Our people are astute. They will notice the change in you. If Brave Hawk and Blue Star arrive tonight, they also will be aware of the change in your attitude. I urge you to make a choice before they arrive. It is for the best benefit of not only you but our people as a whole—as well as Blue Star."

"You are right," Night Wolf said. He swept her into his arms and hugged her. "Thank you for being understanding."

"I am always here for you," Moon Song said, easing from his arms. She rested a hand on his cheek. "Go to the solace of your lodge. Pray to *Wenebojo*. Then you will come to the right decision."

He nodded, took one last look at the young braves at play with the marbles, then went to his lodge.

He slid a log onto the glowing coals of the fire and sat down. He stared at the flames wrapping around the log in a slow caress.

He had a duty as chief, but didn't he have a duty to the woman he loved? Wouldn't it be a service to Marissa to take her away from a life with a father who was unkind? From someone who held such prejudice in his heart toward a man, toward a people, whose skin was not the same color as his?

"I must make up my mind," he whispered.

Ay-uh, he had to decide what to do, and soon.

Blue Star might arrive at any moment.

Chapter 11

Dusk was deepening. The sky was a crimson flush as the sun hung low over the mountains, alerting Marissa that she could not take much longer in her search for the Cree village. She was very aware of the distant howls of a pack of wolves, of the hoots of an owl.

She continued onward across the rolling grassland that gave way to scattered groves of cottonwood. The sweet, heady aroma of honeysuckle wafted on the breeze.

The sunflowers in a field on her left were nodding, dropping their faces earthward, as if the wind had put them to sleep. Pink clover spotted the ground in ragged shreds.

Marissa's white steed's hooves plowed through clumps of buffalo grass, scattering grasshoppers in all directions, another reminder that it was autumn.

She saw the shine of the river beyond and made her way toward it. She had been told that if she followed the river, it would eventually take her to the Cree village.

She wanted to get there before nightfall, if only to get one glimpse of the village, in hopes of seeing the handsome chief.

She doubted that he would ever want to see her again.

Surely her father's insults had hardened Chief Night Wolf not only against her father, but against his daughter as well. He might think that if her blood was the same as her father's, she also harbored prejudices against the red man, even though she had not shown any to him today.

Perhaps Night Wolf thought that their time together had not been all that long and that one could not discover one's true personality in such a short time. Yet she had discovered his, and what a gentle and caring man he was.

Somehow she had to find a way to talk with him again, to set things right with him. She wanted to apologize for the terrible actions of her father.

But she had more than apologies on her mind. Her world had just been changed by what her father had told Bradley.

Her entire life had been a lie.

Her father was not her father. Her mother

was not her mother. Her mother was an Indian. She had been abandoned after her birth.

How could anyone do such a thing? How could a woman carry a child within her womb for nine long months, nourish the child within her, only to leave her to die alone, without love?

And what about her true father?

Had he even known that her mother was pregnant? Would he have wanted Marissa? Would he have saved her from the forest and given her his name?

Suddenly her thoughts were stilled as she saw the Indian village not far in the distance.

She drew a tight rein beside the river and gaped openly at the large camp of tepees. The Cree had erected their skin lodges in a heavy-timbered bottom on the banks of the river, deeply embedded in the surrounding bluffs, which broke the wind and made the long winters more tolerable.

Smoke from the many lodge fires hung in the air over the village, and a great field of corn at the far side lay in straight rows in the path of the sinking sun, brown and ready for harvesting. When the wind moved through the corn, the stalks rattled like old bones.

Marissa wanted to get closer, but she knew that she shouldn't have come this far at this late hour.

And what if someone from the village saw her? Would they see her as an enemy, spying on them? Or would they be as friendly to her as Night Wolf had been and invite her to sit beside the large outdoor fire? Marissa wondered if the fire was for a celebration, or perhaps to ward off animals that might come sniffing around the lodges.

She wanted to go on into the village. Night Wolf lived there, and perhaps her mother was also Cree. Tears filled Marissa's eyes. The need to know the truth about her mother and why she had left her plagued her.

Although Marissa ached to know her mother, she was not certain that her mother would want to know her. Or if her mother still lived.

Yet she could not help herself. She rode closer, by the tall aspen trees, and peered into the village.

She saw children running and playing. A huddle of young braves knelt in a circle, playing a game. Women came from the river, carrying large jugs filled with water. On the far side of the village, a brave walked from the forest, a dead deer slung over his shoulder.

Marissa looked for Night Wolf among the warriors who were busy doing their chores for the village. Her heart skipped a beat when she saw a cluster of older women gathering before a tepee. They were the age her mother would now be.

Had she ever confided in anyone what she had done? Had they known of her betrayal of her Indian husband? Had she been punished, and if so, how? Was she even still alive?

Marissa's questions were running rampant in her head, but they suddenly stopped when she saw him.

Night Wolf.

He went to the fire and threw some fat pieces of wood into the flames. As the fire's glow washed over his muscled body, Marissa's heart melted.

She longed to go to him, to tell him what she had discovered about herself, but she couldn't. Surely he wouldn't want anything to do with her, especially after the way her father had behaved toward him.

Tears spilled from her eyes as Marissa wheeled her horse around and rode back to the mission instead of her cabin. She knew that she could confide anything in Father Mulvaney. He had become a fast, loyal friend, someone she adored and loved. If anyone could guide her about what to do, Father Mulvaney could.

She dismounted before the mission and secured her horse to the hitching rail. She looked toward her home to see if her father had seen her arrival, then went inside the mission.

She walked to the back, where Father Mulvaney had a private office, and found the door open. Father Mulvaney was at his large oak desk, going over entries in a ledger that lay open before him.

When he heard her footsteps, he looked up and gave her a half smile. "Your father has been here more than once to see if you had come here," he said, pushing his chair back. "Marissa, you had all of us worried. You know better than to take off like that."

Marissa smiled softly, sat down in a plush leather chair in front of the desk, then smoothed her windblown hair.

"I didn't mean to worry anyone," she said. "But after what I discovered about myself . . . I . . . had to be alone." She looked over her shoulder to the window that faced her home, then turned to Father Mulvaney again. "Is Father terribly worried?"

"You know the answer to that," the priest said, slowly nodding. "Marissa, I know everything. Your father confided in me after you left. I urged him to go after you."

"Yet he did not try to stop me," Marissa said, her voice breaking.

"No, he did not," Father Mulvaney said. "He said that he felt you needed this time alone, even though he worries about you riding on land that is unfamiliar to you. He doesn't like for you to be this independent."

"I am so confused about so many things," Marissa said, fighting the urge to cry. "It is not only what I discovered about who my true mother is, it is something more than that." She hung her head, then looked up at Father Mulvaney again. "I probably shouldn't tell you . . ."

"I am here to listen," Father Mulvaney said, moving his chair closer to his desk, resting his arms on it. "I will not repeat anything that you confide in me."

"Father Mulvaney, although it might seem strange and sudden, I have fallen in love with the Cree chief," she blurted out. "I have fallen in love with Night Wolf!"

She saw the shock that registered in Father Mulvaney's eyes. She was aware of his silence as he gazed in amazement at her.

"Please say something," she said, searching his eyes. "Is what I said so horrible . . . so wrong?"

"No, my dear. Please do not interpret my silence as anything bad," Father Mulvaney said, rising from his chair. His long black robe swirled around his legs as he stepped around the desk and reached for Marissa's hands. When she twined her fingers in his, he urged her to her feet.

He held her in a gentle embrace, where she found such comfort, such peace.

He hugged her for a moment longer, then stepped away from her, and held her hands. "My dear, it is not shameful or wrong to love an Indian chief," he said. "It was your father who was wrong to show such prejudice toward a wonderful man. Night Wolf is a gentle, lovable man whom everyone admires."

"My father doesn't," Marissa said. "I think he hates him."

"He doesn't hate him," Father Mulvaney said. "He just sees him as a threat. Your father has guarded your identity for so long, I believe he thought that if you became involved with the Cree, you might discover the truth yourself."

"He told the truth to Bradley Coomer, yet not to me," Marissa said, unable to hold back sobs. "He had to know that if he told Bradley, Bradley would tell me. And if Bradley knew, the whole world would soon know. That man doesn't have a trace of decency in him. He is not a man that can be trusted with anything, especially such a secret as this."

"Your father told me that he had decided to tell you the truth, as well," Father Mulvaney said. "If he never wanted you to know the truth, he shouldn't have taken you from your home in Kansas. I shall never understand why he did not think of the consequences of such a decision."

"The consequences of his daughter discovering her true heritage and falling in love with a powerful Cree chief," Marissa said, with a sigh. "I do love Night Wolf, Father. What can I do? How can one love so much, and so quickly, yet have that love denied to her?"

"There is more than your father to stand in the way of that love," Father Mulvaney said. He motioned her to sit down, then sat behind his desk again. "My dear, I have something to tell you that will only make things worse, yet you have to know. It is a shame that you fell so instantly in love with Night Wolf, for he is not available for the taking."

Marissa felt the blood drain from her face.

"What do you mean?" she asked, feeling a slow ache beginning in her heart. "Is . . . he . . . married? He never told me he was married."

"No, he isn't married," Father Mulvaney said, seeing the relief rush into Marissa's eyes. "But he is promised to someone else—a woman called Blue Star."

It was as though someone had splashed cold water onto her face. The reality of what Father Mulvaney had just told her was heartbreaking.

She hung her head as she fought off tears, then sought courage deep within herself.

"He . . . is . . . promised to another?" she murmured, her eyes meeting and holding Father Mulvaney's. She clamped a hand over her mouth to hold back the renewed sobs.

How could Night Wolf have become this important to her so quickly? Why did knowing that she could never share anything with him again hurt so badly?

She was confused by everything that she had found out today. She had been denied her true birthright by a mother who did not want her. Now she was denied a man she had such deep feelings for. Her world seemed to be turned upside down, and she did not know if it could ever be right again.

Father Mulvaney saw her despair, urged her to her feet and again gave her a comforting hug.

"My dear, you must forget these feelings," he said. "Marissa, consider giving yourself up to the Lord and becoming a nun. Nothing is more rewarding than giving one's life to the work of the Lord."

Marissa eased out of his arms. "Father Mulvaney, I understand what you are trying to do for me and I appreciate it," she said. "And I respect you with all my heart. But I can't be a nun. I don't have the desire that should be there for someone to give her life to the Lord's work. I have the longings of a woman who needs a man—and not just any man. Night Wolf. Although he is not mine to have, I love him no less."

"Marissa, you *must* forget him," Father Mulvaney said firmly. "Your feelings for him are wrong, even . . . sinful. You should not be wanting another woman's man. Repent! Go home, Marissa. Take solace in prayer."

Feeling that everything had gone wrong today, Marissa backed slowly away from him.

She searched his eyes, then smiled weakly. "Thank you for talking with me," she said.

She turned quickly and fled the mission. She grabbed her horse's reins and took him to the small livery stable that her father had built, before rushing into the house. She did not stop until she reached the privacy of her room.

Her father knew that she was home. She had seen him standing by lamplight at his study window, watching her.

She knew that she should go to him. He had probably seen her go to the mission to confide in Father Mulvaney, when she should have been talking things over with him instead. She did not want to hurt him, regardless of the hurt he had caused her. She needed time alone. She would pray, and then go and talk with her father. She must know everything about that day she was found.

And she must find a way to remove Night Wolf from her heart.

"Blue Star," she thought to herself. "Could Night Wolf truly love Blue Star, yet show such affection toward me at the same time?"

She buried her face in her hands. "Stop this!" she whispered to herself. "You must stop this!"

Chapter 12

The moon was high and bright in the sky. In the distance coyotes yelped and owls hooted. Night Wolf tied his reins to a low tree limb, then kept in the shadows as he ran around to the back of the cabin where he had seen Marissa standing at a window earlier that day.

He was glad that the fort was far enough away from the trading post so the sentries could not detect him in the darkness. The lamplight was out at the mission, which meant the priests were asleep. He moved stealthily onward through the night with quick panther movements and soon stood just outside Marissa's bedroom.

He wanted to know her better and hoped she might come out in the moonlight and talk with him. He had brought her a gift as a sign of friendship.

He had thought long and hard about his feelings. He needed to discover if his first reaction to her was true, that she was a sweet and caring person. And if she was, what then of Blue Star and his promise to marry her? How could he love one woman and marry another? What honesty was there in that? None.

Hoping that soon all of these questions would be answered, he stepped closer to the window.

Lamplight flowed softly through the glass of the window. He peered through it and looked around the room. It was interesting to see how Marissa lived, since he had never seen a white woman's private room before.

Everything about it was vastly different from the way the women of his village lived. He gazed at the lace-trimmed canopy on her bed and the matching pillows and bedspread that just barely brushed the wooden floor.

Her bedside table held a lamp. Its light glimmered from a wick inside a small glass chimney, revealing numerous books lying beside it. He gathered that Marissa was a well-educated woman, who had probably attended schools in the city where she had lived.

Disappointed that he had not found her there, he continued surveying the room, intrigued by the things he saw. At the foot of the bed sat a massive trunk. It was open, revealing dainty clothes draped around the edges, all pretty in color and make.

He wondered what she would think about the clothes his tribe's women wore. The doeskin was as white as a winter snowfall, and the beautiful multi-colored beads were sewn on by those who owned them.

He could envision Marissa in white, with beads draped around her throat and on her wrist and her black hair worn in one long braid down her back.

He shook himself to stop such thoughts. He had come tonight with a purpose, and it was obvious that he would not achieve his goal. She was not there. Their talk, which might have settled things within his heart, would be delayed until another time.

He looked down at the moccasins in his hands. He had brought Marissa a pair made by the most skilled Cree women of his village. They were of soft doeskin and had a design of turquoise beads on the top.

He truly believed that Marissa would enjoy having such a gift. He looked at the windowsill, then at the moccasins. He set them on the ground beside him, then slowly raised the window. His heart pounding, he put the moccasins on the ledge of the windowsill, wondering how Marissa might react when she saw them there.

Would it frighten her to know that someone had been there, peering through the window? Or would she know that it was not just anyone who had brought her a gift? Would she know that it was Night Wolf who cared enough to bring them to her?

Their time together had been short, yet it had been enough for him to know that what had been exchanged between them was almost mystical. He knew that he would never forget it. He hoped fervently that she would never forget him.

The moccasins left behind, he moved stealthily onward, keeping himself in the shadow of the cabin. He went from window to window, seeking her out. He finally saw her sitting with her father in a room of many books, which lined shelves on a far wall. His heart stopped as he saw what her father was handing her.

Night Wolf's eyes widened when Marissa held a tiny necklace out before her, looking at it and studying it while her father talked to her.

Night Wolf recognized the style of the necklace. It resembled the one that Shame on Face wore every day. It was made of the same rare blue beads that Shame on Face had brought from her home in the Minnesota territory when she married her Cree warrior and traveled here to live with him amid his people.

Surely Marissa's father had acquired this necklace by trading for it. How else would he have it? And why was he showing it to Marissa?

He watched as Marissa and her father continued to talk. They were so serious. Marissa seemed in awe of what her father was telling her. As she held the tiny necklace in one hand, she embraced her father.

Whatever had caused her father to be so angry with Marissa earlier now seemed to have been forgiven and forgotten. Night Wolf was watching a father and daughter who loved one another and who appeared to have settled their differences.

And it all seemed centered on the necklace.

After her father's prejudicial reaction to seeing her with Night Wolf, why would an Indian necklace be so valuable to both Marissa and her father?

Already torn over his feelings for Marissa, and now puzzled by her father's changing behavior, Night Wolf ran quietly back to his horse, then rode away into the darkness.

Now more than ever he wanted to uncover the mystery of this woman. And he would!

The necklace haunted him. What connection was there between Marissa and the necklace? And why did it look identical to Shame on Face's?

Chapter 13

Marissa went to her bedroom and closed her door. Contemplating what had just happened between herself and her father, she walked slowly into the room, then stopped and stared down at her hand. Her fingers curled around the only thing that could possibly prove who she was.

After coming to terms with the fact that she was adopted instead of being the birth daughter of her parents, she felt blessed to have had such a wonderful mother and father to care for her. No matter that they had not given birth to her. Marissa felt closer tonight to her father and her beloved mother than ever before.

To know that they could give up their lives to take Marissa away from the wilderness to protect her from harm made Marissa feel humble and appreciative toward her parents.

No daughter could have been as loved as

she. No parents could have been as attentive. She had been given everything a girl would want. She had had love, a wonderful home, schooling.

Nothing could ever change the love she felt for her father. At this moment she could not love him any more. He was not only a father, he was a friend.

Yet there was still that part of her that wanted to find her true parents, especially her mother. She had to know why she had abandoned her baby, how she could have done such a thing.

She wanted to know how her mother had lived with what she had done.

Marissa had decided to seek answers.

"And the necklace," she whispered as she held her hand out and slowly uncurled her fingers.

Once again she gazed at the tiny thing that lay in her palm. She knew it was a bond between herself and her birth mother.

If she could discover the woman who recognized the necklace, then she would have found her mother.

Yes, she *would* search for answers. Her father knew that she would. He was not happy about it, yet he knew her feelings and he understood. He had not actually given her his blessing, but she knew that he would not lock her in her room to keep her from doing it.

Suddenly something caught her eye. Her heart skipped a beat. She slid the necklace into her pocket and walked guardedly toward the open window. She could not believe what she saw sitting there on the ledge.

The lovely doeskin moccasins sent a sweet message to Marissa's heart, for they had surely been left there by Night Wolf. She was deeply touched by the gift and longed to see and talk with him.

But she had to remind herself of what Father Mulvaney had said. Night Wolf was not free to have feelings for her. He had made an agreement that another woman would soon be his wife.

She looked quickly through the window. What if he was watching her, awaiting her reaction? She lifted the moccasins lovingly from the windowsill, held them to her heart and smiled. Hoping that he was still out there, she set them aside, crawled through the window, and walked in the moonlight, her eyes searching through the darkness.

"Are you here?" she asked, hoping that no one but he would hear her. She didn't want her father to know that she was out there searching for the handsome Indian chief. He still would never accept her feelings about Night Wolf.

She was disappointed when she didn't find Night Wolf anywhere. He must have arrived while she had been discussing things with her father. When he found her gone, he left the gift so she would know that he had been there, had been thinking about her.

"I must not want him," she whispered to herself.

No, she shouldn't think about him. Yet there was something more than desire now. Maybe Night Wolf could help with her questions about her Indian mother. If he saw the necklace, would it mean anything to him? Would he recognize it?

Unable to stop herself, Marissa determinedly went to the livery stable. Her father's lamplight was out at his window. He had gone to bed for the night.

She saddled her horse and daringly left beneath the light of the orange harvest moon.

Chapter 14

Even before Night Wolf entered his village he knew that Brave Hawk and the Chippewa people had arrived. He saw the Chippewa canoes beached at the river. They were still loaded with supplies.

The drone of voices wafted to him through the air, and he knew that everyone was around the large outdoor fire, renewing old acquaintances and making new ones.

Night Wolf halted his horse and waited a moment before riding on into his village. He was about to come face-to-face with Blue Star, his intended. He did not doubt her loveliness. It was just that he no longer felt that he could agree to the marriage. So much depended on it—most of all, his honor. An honorable man stood behind his promises, especially to a woman.

But did not an honorable man also answer to the beckoning of his heart?

Sighing, knowing that he was only delaying the inevitable, Night Wolf sank his heels into the flanks of his strawberry roan and rode into his village. Everyone became quiet and watched his approach.

The moon was high in the sky, giving off a soft white light that revealed faces he scarcely remembered. He recognized Brave Hawk and the warriors who had joined the large council some moons ago during a meeting of tribes.

As Brave Hawk stepped away from the crowd and walked toward Night Wolf, Night Wolf dismounted and met his friend halfway. Their embrace was quick and sincere.

"It has been too long," Brave Hawk said, stepping back, his hand on Night Wolf's shoulder. "It is good to be here. The journey was not without mishap. We traveled as much as we could on water, then carried our canoes. It was tiring. We ride horses well enough, but our main mode of travel is canoe."

"Had I known when you were definitely coming, I could have met you halfway," Night Wolf said, aware of a lovely woman walking toward him. She had snapping black eyes, a long black braid down her back, and was clad in beaded doeskin. A long string of beads hung from her bare neck, and she had tiny, yet snugly moccasined feet.

Her facial features were flawless, a face that he could easily have loved. Still, when he thought of a bride, he did not see her.

He saw Marissa.

He tensed when Blue Star stepped up beside her brother, her black eyes slowly assessing Night Wolf, as his had just assessed her. He was uneasy under such scrutiny, but only because he knew that she was looking at him as her future husband. He would find it hard to reveal the truth to both her and Brave Hawk, but he must. He could not carry out this deceit. He had to find a way to tell Brave Hawk and Blue Star that though a pact had been made, things had changed and the agreement would have to be severed.

Even before seeing Blue Star as a ravishingly beautiful maiden, he had made his decision.

He had chosen Marissa.

"Night Wolf, it has been many, many moons since you saw my sister, Blue Star," Brave Hawk said. He swept an arm around his sister's waist and drew her closer to him. "But you see her now. Did I tell you that you would not be disappointed? Is she not as beautiful as I promised? Has she not grown from the child you knew so long ago into a woman that will make a good wife for a powerful chief?"

Night Wolf felt his heart thumping wildly

within his chest. He was finding it hard to listen to words that he knew were no longer true. He was not going to marry Blue Star. He could not give his heart falsely to a woman. It would not be fair to him, or to the woman whom he could never love.

He studied Brave Hawk and Blue Star. He saw in their eyes their eagerness for this union. He had to depend on the friendship he had shared with Brave Hawk for so long to make him understand.

"*Ay-uh*, she is *mee-kah-wah-diz-ee*, beautiful," Night Wolf said finally when he saw their questioning looks. "She will make a wonderful wife."

Blue Star smiled brightly, making Night Wolf feel very deceitful. He had not meant that she would make *him* a wonderful wife. He hoped he would find a way to make them understand why this never could be.

"Let us go and join everyone around the fire," Night Wolf said.

He smelled the fragrance of the food that had been prepared in celebration of an alliance between the two strong bands of people. He hoped that his decision would not cause that bond to break, and that his people would understand that his heart belonged to someone other than the woman he had promised to marry.

Night Wolf saw Shame on Face leave her tepee holding Moon Song and his mother's hand. He felt a gladness sweep through him to see Shame on Face brought from her hiding.

The Chippewa were her people. She had not seen them since she had left to join her Cree husband's village.

When he had abandoned her she had chosen not to return to them. Instead she kept herself hidden in shame. Now by her look of happiness, he wondered if she regretted her decision.

But that was then. This was now. She could begin her life anew. She no longer had to hide in her tepee but could join those who loved her then, and who still loved her now.

Night Wolf settled down on a blanket with Brave Hawk on one side and Blue Star on the other. He was uncomfortable with how close Blue Star sat to him, as though she were already his wife. He moved farther away from her. As the large platter of food was brought to him, Night Wolf directed his conversation to Brave Hawk.

He was not aware that Blue Star was feeling left out. She got up and ran from the village, stopping at the riverbank with tears in her eyes.

She fell to her knees, and held her face over the water. Blue Star gazed at her reflection as the moon spilled its sheen into the river, giving her enough light to see.

"Am I not pretty enough for him?" she whispered as she studied her features.

Her brother had constantly told her that she was beautiful, that she was flawless.

Then why was Night Wolf purposely avoiding her? She was promised to him. Did he not want her? Had he seen something about her that had displeased him?

She had been counting in her heart the sleeps before she would finally be with Night Wolf. Now that she was, had he chosen not to marry her after all?

The snapping of a twig behind her made her smile. Surely Night Wolf had seen her leave and had come for her. Her pulse racing, she turned her head to see. She rushed to her feet and looked guardedly at a white woman who came into sight at the edge of the forest.

"Who are you?" Blue Star asked in the English language that she had learned as a child.

"My name is Marissa," Marissa said, stunned by the woman's loveliness. She had never seen such a beautiful woman. She made Marissa feel unattractive.

"I have come as a friend," Marissa added quickly. "Could we speak as friends speak?"

Marissa wanted to get answers tonight. Perhaps this woman knew someone at the Cree village who might have abandoned a child. Of course she knew the chances of that were small. But she had to start somewhere.

"Yes, we can speak as friends," Blue Star said, relaxing her shoulders. "Why are you alone in the night? Do you feel safe being here alone? Where have you come from? How did you get here? By canoe?"

"No, I didn't come by canoe," Marissa said. "I have my horse. I tethered it beneath the trees over yonder. Do you ride horses?"

"Yes, but I do not own any," Blue Star said. She nodded toward the many beached canoes. "My favorite mode of travel is canoe."

Marissa looked past Blue Star. Her eyebrows rose when she saw the canoes. They were filled with supplies. She wondered why. Had visitors come to the Cree village?

She did hear laughter and conversation coming from the direction of the outdoor fire. She had not gone to look before seeing this woman alone at the river.

"I have met your chief," Marissa murmured. "I know him."

"How could you have met my brother, the

chief?" Blue Star asked. "He is new to this area."

Marissa's eyes widened. "You are Night Wolf's sister? He is new to the area? I thought that he had lived here for many years."

"No, I do not speak of Night Wolf," Blue Star said, now looking guardedly at Marissa. "My brother is Brave Hawk. We are Chippewa. We arrived tonight to live with the Cree as one people. We are making a strong alliance."

"Really?" Marissa said, looking at Blue Star more closely.

"My name is Blue Star," she said, proudly squaring her shoulders. "I will soon be married to Chief Night Wolf."

Marissa was so stunned that she couldn't speak. She was face-to-face with the very woman who would soon be speaking vows with Night Wolf. The woman who would be sleeping with him, who would be bearing his children.

Knowing this, and seeing how beautiful Blue Star was, Marissa felt trapped. She had come to seek answers, but these weren't the sort of answers she had wanted to know. Who would have guessed that she would come upon the very woman she could not help but be jealous of?

Marissa knew that no matter what she did or

said, Night Wolf could never turn his back on such loveliness.

"I must go," Marissa said, backing slowly away from Blue Star. "Truly—I must go."

"You said that you wanted to talk as friends, yet you leave so quickly?" Blue Star said. "Can we meet again? It would be good to have a friend. You can show me the interesting places of this land. I would like to know everything, since I am to be the wife of the chief."

Marissa was uncertain. She saw how eager this woman was to have her as a friend, and understood her reasons. Blue Star wanted to learn about the land so that she could show Night Wolf that she knew it before he could introduce her to it. It was a clever scheme, one that Marissa truly did not want to be a part of.

Yet if she turned Blue Star down, she might become Marissa's enemy. And Marissa could use her friendship to her own advantage. In time, Blue Star would learn about everyone in the village. She wanted to impress Night Wolf, and learning about his people and becoming acquainted with them would be another way to prove her worth to this man.

If Blue Star learned about everyone, could not she share this with Marissa? In time she might help Marissa discover who her true mother was.

"Yes, I will be glad to show you the land," Marissa said, deciding to set her own plan in motion. "First I would like to introduce you to Father Mulvaney at the mission. He is a kind man. You will enjoy knowing him."

"Explain to me how to get to the mission," Blue Star said. She understood these men of God, for several had settled close to her village back in the Minnesota Territory. As long as they did not try to force their religion on the Chippewa, they had been welcomed.

She had befriended one in particular who was younger than the others. He had taught her many things about the white world, especially the love of horses. He had a snow-white steed. She had felt so special riding it.

She already missed Father Scott Taylor. Even though he was a priest, she had fallen in love with him, as had he with her. But for many reasons that love was forbidden.

So she centered her attention on marrying Night Wolf.

Marissa explained how to get to the mission. "Come in the morning," she said. "We shall have a good day."

She did not tell Blue Star that they must do all of their socializing away from Marissa's father. It was something this Chippewa maiden would not understand, especially since Marissa did not understand it herself.

"*Ay-uh*, a good day," Blue Star said.

"I must go," Marissa said. "I have been gone for too long as it is."

"Your family worries about you being alone in the dark?" Blue Star said as she walked Marissa to her horse.

"My father does not allow it at all," Marissa said with a pinched look. "I came after he went to sleep."

"Why did you come to the Cree village?" Blue Star asked.

Marissa's spine stiffened. Having no choice but to lie, Marissa answered, "I was riding. I saw you standing alone. I wanted to make your acquaintance."

Blue Star hugged Marissa. "It is good to know you," she said, then, smiling, she stepped away.

"You, too," Marissa said, then mounted her steed.

"I shall arrive tomorrow on one of Night Wolf's horses," Blue Star said. "I love horses, although my people do not own any. A mission of white priests sat close to our village. They had a few. Father Scott Taylor taught me to ride."

"Then you already know the goodness of the

priests," Marissa said. "You will love Father Mulvaney."

She wheeled her horse around, gave Blue Star a final wave, then rode away.

When she got far enough from Blue Star and the village, she halted her horse and held her face in her hands and cried. Tonight she had made friends with the very woman that Night Wolf would soon marry.

How could she continue this friendship? It would hurt deeply every time Marissa was around Blue Star. It would hurt whenever Blue Star talked about Night Wolf, perhaps even confiding details of their wedding night together.

"Is he in love with her?" Marissa whispered out loud, lifting her eyes toward the shine of the outdoor fire.

Why had he left the moccasins?

She had felt that they were a message. A message she had taken inside her heart and savored.

Puzzled, she rode toward home.

Chapter 15

As the morning wore on, the Cree village was busy with its usual activities. Some of the women carried hoes made of buffalo bone to the surrounding hills to dig for wild turnips. Others remained in camp, fleshing new antelope skins or catching up with their quillwork and beading. The Chippewa women, who were now a part of the village, were shown the daily routine, and the two groups spent time talking and comparing how chores were done.

Night Wolf was helping to construct tepees for the Chippewa. Although they normally lived in wigwams—structures made of round, bent poles covered with bulrush mats—the winters out west were much too harsh for that sort of dwelling. They would need the warmth and security of buffalo hide tepees.

Brave Hawk worked alongside Night Wolf. Uneasy over Brave Hawk's quiet demeanor and his lingering glances, Night Wolf laid aside the pole that he had started to plant in the ground and turned to his friend.

Brave Hawk met Night Wolf's steady gaze with one of his own.

"My friend, there seems to be some tension between us," Night Wolf said. "Usually when we work side by side, we talk. Today our time together is spent in silence. I have felt your eyes on me. Do you wish to tell me what is bothering you?"

Brave Hawk brushed back a thick strand of hair that had fallen from his beaded headband, before nodding.

"*Ay-uh*, yes," Brave Hawk said. "I feel that something between us is not right."

"And what do you think it is?" Night Wolf asked, fearing that his friend could see into his heart and not see his sister there.

"That is not for me to say," Brave Hawk said tightly. "Is there something you hesitate to tell me?"

Brave Hawk had noticed how Night Wolf seemed to avoid his sister. He had hoped for a wedding soon after their arrival. How could there be a wedding if the man does not look at the bride with favor in his eyes? It had been many winters since Night Wolf had seen Blue Star. She had grown into maturity now. She was a vivacious, beautiful woman. How could any man look at her and not want her?

He hoped that he was wrong, and that his friend's behavior had another origin, one that had nothing to do with the arrival of Blue Star in his life.

The question unsettled Night Wolf. He looked over his shoulder at the peacefulness of his village. The Chippewa and the Cree were working side by side, laughing, and enjoying being together.

Many years ago, Night Wolf's chieftain father had uprooted his Cree people and taken them to a land where buffalo roamed in hordes. Now those people were reunited. The alliance that Night Wolf had dreamed of was there today, strong and vital. It was everything that he had wished it to be.

Yet, there was one obstacle that might erase all of the happiness. If he turned his back on Blue Star and chose the white woman, how would everyone respond?

But he had made up his mind. He knew that he could not live without Marissa, regardless of her father's prejudices toward him.

He was not ready to answer questions that might throw everything into a whirlwind of distrust and anger.

"Is there something in particular that you

think is causing problems between us?" Night Wolf asked instead of responding truthfully to Brave Hawk's question.

Brave Hawk was taken aback by Night Wolf's reluctance to answer him. He now, more than ever, believed that his friend's strange behavior involved Blue Star.

Brave Hawk's jaw stiffened. He had too much pride to continue this game with his friend. If Night Wolf was not ready to give him the truth, so be it. Brave Hawk would not demand answers. He would wait and watch.

"*Gah-ween*, no, there is nothing particular on my mind," Brave Hawk said, searching his friend's eyes.

He wanted this alliance with Night Wolf regardless of how he might feel about Blue Star. The marriage would be the best thing for her, even if Night Wolf had changed his mind about the arrangement. Even if Blue Star would rather be marrying someone else anyway.

Father Scott Taylor was a young priest who had grown close to the band of Chippewa. Although Father Taylor was a man of God, Brave Hawk knew that he had fallen in love with Blue Star and she with him.

It was the main reason that Brave Hawk had been anxious to leave the land of many lakes. He knew it was best to sever all ties with Father

Taylor, for the longer he was around Blue Star, the more it would hurt her.

Brave Hawk could not confide any of this to Night Wolf. The name Father Taylor must not be spoken again. The longer his sister was away from him, the sooner she might be able to forget.

"Then if you are comfortable with things as they are between us, I hope you understand I have to leave," Night Wolf said, placing a hand on Brave Hawk's shoulder. "I have business elsewhere, a private council. But if you wish to wait for me, I will help you finish this tepee another time."

"*Gah-ween*, no, do not hurry with your council because of an unfinished tepee," Brave Hawk said. Something about Night Hawk's demeanor was puzzling. He had not spoken of any planned council earlier.

"I will be gone for only a short while. When I return, I wish a private council with you," Night Wolf said, slowly lowering his hand to his side.

Brave Hawk's insides tightened. "Does this have to do with my sister?" he blurted, and immediately wished that he didn't.

Taken aback by the question, Night Wolf did not respond right away.

After a moment, he said, "Yes, but I want to wait and talk about Blue Star when I return."

"I will look for your return," Brave Hawk replied. "My *gee-gee-kee-wayn-gee*, brother, I look forward to our council."

Night Wolf sensed that Brave Hawk understood all too well about his feelings. His friend had always been astute, especially when it was something between two old friends.

He quickly embraced Brave Hawk. "It is so good to have you here with me and my people," he said. "Although we are not blood brothers, we are brothers no less."

"Yes, brothers for always," Brave Hawk said, returning the hug.

Inhaling deeply, Night Wolf stepped away from Brave Hawk. They clasped hands and nodded, then Night Wolf hurried to his horse, which was saddled and ready. He knew that he would go to speak with Marissa today whether or not her father approved.

He rode from the village with his chin held high and his shoulders squared. When he returned, his role as chief might be tested. It depended on whether or not he would reveal the truth to his people who now included the Chippewa.

He rode past golden aspens, across fields of purple clover, and beneath the shadow of an eagle soaring overhead. Night Wolf did not feel guilty about having lost his battle with his heart. He was in love with Marissa. No matter how hard he tried, he couldn't get her off his mind. When he closed his eyes, her face was there. When he dreamed, Marissa was in his arms, her sweet lips pressed against his.

He could not turn his back on a love that was true. He laughed to himself when he thought of how he had hoped to discover something about Marissa that would make it easy to forget her and accept Blue Star into his heart. He doubted there was anything about Marissa that could turn his heart away from her. In the short time they had been together, everything about her had come to him like a sweet song.

As he approached the trading post from the forests, he saw Marissa leaving through the back door, heading toward the mission.

She was alone.

He rode toward her, the horse's hoofbeats loud. She gazed in wonder as Night Wolf approached.

Night Wolf stopped beneath a tall aspen. He dismounted and secured his reins to a low limb, then went to Marissa. Her eyes never left him.

He could see her pulse beating rapidly in the

tiny vein at her throat and knew that his presence was the cause.

"Did you find the moccasins?" he asked softly, his eyes searching hers.

Marissa was amazed that Night Wolf had come in the middle of the morning, in broad daylight. He had to know that her father could appear at any moment and order him away.

"Yes, I found the moccasins," she murmured, smiling sweetly at him. "Are you the one who placed them at my window?"

"Yes, I am the one," Night Wolf said, so eager to reach for her and hold her, as he had thought so often of doing. "Did you approve? I had hoped to talk with you."

"You had?" Marissa asked, her eyes widening. "Even though my father—my father was so crude in his behavior toward you?"

"Your father is mistaken about many things," Night Wolf said. "He was reacting to his daughter being with a stranger—and not just any stranger but an Indian."

"Yes, he was quite disturbed over my being with you," Marissa said. She lowered her eyes, then gazed at him again. "I apologize for my father's rudeness. I hope that in time he will see the wrong in it."

Night Wolf reached out for her and was glad when she didn't step away from him. He gently touched her face, enjoying the softness of her skin. "You know as well as I that his prejudice is toward my feelings for you, nothing more," he said. "I talked with him only moments before, and he was friendly and cordial. He is a father who does not want his white daughter to have feelings for a man with my color of skin."

"I believe that is true, sadly," Marissa answered. Her heart was thudding and her knees weakened as he continued to touch her face.

She knew that she should step away from Night Wolf, just in case her father might look out the window or come out of the back door, but she was held by the look in Night Wolf's eyes.

Night Wolf looked toward the shadows of the forest, then gazed at Marissa again.

"Can we go where we cannot be seen so readily?" he asked. "I have something to say to you and I do not want your father to be a witness to it."

Marissa nodded. "Yes, let's," she said.

She walked quickly with him deeper into the shadows. Her heart soared when he suddenly placed his arms around her waist and drew her close to him.

"White woman, do you not know that you have stolen my heart?" he said, his eyes searching hers. "I cannot help but to want and love you. It happened the very morning we met. It was our destiny. Remember the butterfly? It was an omen. A good omen."

Finding it all so incredible, Marissa was speechless. The man she adored had just professed his love for her.

She wanted to admit her true feelings to him, but he was promised to another woman. Blue Star was supposed to be his wife. All of this was wrong.

Her thoughts were swept away as he pulled her closer. His arms held her tightly against him as he lowered his lips and kissed her. The passion between them was so vivid that she could not help but return the kiss. She twined her arms around his neck and pressed her body against his.

The front door at the mission slammed shut, and out of the corner of her eye she saw Father Mulvaney walking toward his garden.

A sudden guilt grabbed at her. She recalled how Father Mulvaney had shamed her for loving a man who belonged to another woman. He had said that it was sinful of her to want Night Wolf. He had told her to repent.

Marissa jerked free of Night Wolf's embrace. She looked up into his eyes and saw the questions, the hurt. She knew that he was not free to love her.

Tears of frustration welled in her eyes.

She stepped away from Night Wolf, then turned quickly and ran hard in the direction of the mission.

Stunned, Night Wolf watched Marissa fall into the priest's arms. Father Mulvaney whisked her inside the mission.

Night Wolf wanted to go after her and ask why she was fighting her feelings, but he knew the answer. She feared her father.

Frowning, he turned and gazed at the trading post. He wanted to go and face the man, yet he did not have the right to. If Marissa wanted Night Wolf, it was her place to make things right with her father.

Until she did so, Night Wolf must make certain that he did not put himself in such a position as he had today. He would not pursue her any longer. But he knew that he could not marry Blue Star either.

His heart weary, Night Wolf mounted his steed and wheeled around to head back in the direction of his village. He took one long, last look at the mission, in hopes of getting another glimpse of Marissa. Seeing no one, he kicked the flanks of his horse and rode at a hard gallop. The wind was welcome on his face. It helped wash away the disappointment that had come with Marissa's denial of him moments ago.

Chapter 16

Blue Star knelt behind the bushes, stunned by what she had just seen. She could not believe that the man she was supposed to marry had kissed another woman. She would never forget the look in Night Wolf's eyes as he watched Marissa run from him.

She waited until Night Wolf disappeared into the shadows of the forest behind the trading post. Feeling betrayed and angry at both Night Wolf and the woman, Blue Star rose slowly to her feet and walked disheartedly back to the horse that she had left hidden behind her. She knelt beside him, her face in her hands. The world was an unkind place. She thought back to this morning. Things had seemed to go awry the moment she saw her brother and Night Wolf erecting a new tepee.

Just before Night Wolf left on his horse, she had seen a strain between them. They were uncharacteristically quiet as they worked. And Night Wolf was purposely avoiding her.

For a man who was to soon marry a woman, he was not showing any signs of affection for Blue Star. They had not discussed when the vows would be spoken between them, nor had they begun making plans for their future together. She was smart enough to know when a man did not want her.

She was afraid that her people had also seen Night Wolf's evasiveness. During their long journey, the tribe talked of little else but the upcoming nuptials between the revered Cree chief and the sister of Brave Hawk.

If the marriage didn't take place, how would Night Wolf and she be perceived? Would her Chippewa people see him as deceitful? Would they see her as a woman who was not lovely enough to capture the Cree chief's heart?

But had she not already captured a man's heart?

"Scott," she whispered to herself, tears splashing from her eyes.

She missed Father Taylor. She and Scott had grown close during their times together. He had taught her to read and write. She fell in love with him, and she knew that he had fallen in love with her. But he had promised himself to his Lord and was not free to love a woman.

Blue Star had been eager to leave the land of many lakes, because being with a man that she could never marry had begun to eat away at her heart.

She had hoped that when she arrived at the Cree village, and married Chief Night Wolf, he would help her forget Scott.

She had remembered Night Wolf from those many years ago when she was a child and he was growing into a handsome young brave. She had secretly loved him then, in her childish way.

But when she had met Father Scott Taylor, she knew a different kind of love. It went deep inside her, where desires were born.

Realizing that her thoughts had strayed from the problem at hand, Blue Star thought back to that morning when the impulse to spy on Night Wolf struck.

Instead of finishing the tepee with Brave Hawk, he had ridden away to the trading post. It was obvious that Night Wolf had not ventured there for trading. She watched from the shadows as he circled the forest and came up behind the building. She watched him tie his reins to a low limb in the dark shadows.

Blue Star had approached from the opposite direction of where he had stopped and she chose a place where she could get a good view.

From her vantage point she wasn't able to see Night Wolf at first. She secured her horse and knelt behind the bushes, waiting to see what he would do.

Her heart leapt into her throat when she saw Night Wolf step from the shadows to talk with the white woman, Marissa, whom Blue Star had met beside the river. Marissa had never told Blue Star exactly why she had come that close to the Cree village, but Blue Star now knew that Marissa had had a purpose—to spy on Night Wolf.

Blue Star watched as Night Wolf and Marissa moved into each other's embrace and kissed. Blue Star then realized why Night Wolf had been avoiding her. He was in love with another woman. Yet that woman had run from him, crying.

She stiffened at the sound of a horse approaching from the woods. Through a break in the trees she saw Night Wolf ride past in the direction of his village. She sighed with relief to know that he had not found her there.

She would never tell anyone what she had witnessed. She would wait and see exactly what Night Wolf's next move would be.

Perhaps Marissa had heard of the upcoming nuptials between Night Wolf and Blue Star. That would explain why she had fiercely embraced Night Wolf one minute, then fled from him the next.

Maybe Night Wolf *was* going to marry Blue Star after all, and the reason he was behaving so strangely was that he knew he had to tell this white woman that he could no longer be with her.

With determination etched on her face, Blue Star watched Marissa and Father Mulvaney emerge from the mission and walk through the garden as they talked. Blue Star grabbed her horse's reins, mounted and rode out from her hiding place.

Marissa and the priest turned when they heard her approaching. Blue Star centered her attention on Marissa, and avoided looking at the priest. His black robe reminded her of another man.

She stopped a few feet from Marissa and Father Mulvaney and directed a seething look toward Marissa.

"White woman, stay away from Night Wolf," Blue Star said in a low hiss. "Night Wolf is my man. We are soon to marry!"

Blue Star glowered at Marissa for a moment longer, then wheeled her horse around and started to ride off. But first she turned and glared at Marissa again. "You and I? We are friends no more!"

Guilt surged through Marissa. She knew that Blue Star must have seen her and Night Wolf embrace and kiss.

Marissa started to run toward her, to try and explain, but a gentle hand on her wrist stopped her.

"Let her go," Father Mulvaney said in his comforting voice. "Things are settled between you. You can go on with your life now. You are a good woman. You have been forgiven. It is all behind you now. All of it."

Marissa stifled a sob, turned to Father Mulvaney, then nodded.

"Yes, it is behind me," she murmured. Then she broke free of his grip and ran to seek the privacy of her room.

She needed to be alone with her thoughts, with her memories of a kiss that would be with her for eternity.

She knew that she could never love anyone but Night Wolf.

In a sense, she would be living a celibate life. She would never marry. Perhaps she should become a nun. That would solve everything.

Chapter 17

Brooding and deep in thought, Night Wolf sat before his lodge fire. He was not ready to have his private council with Brave Hawk. He was still unnerved and confused about Marissa's attitude toward him after they had kissed. In their embrace, he had found the paradise that he had known would come with being with Marissa.

He knew without a doubt that his heart was hers and could never belong to anyone else. He knew that her heart belonged to him. Yet she had run from him.

"What am I to do?" he whispered, raking his long, lean fingers through his raven-black hair.

He was a powerful chief who should not be distracted by anything. His thoughts should be centered on his people, not on a woman.

He had a duty to Brave Hawk as well. He must explain to his friend that he could not marry his sister, regardless that Marissa had turned her back on Night Wolf today.

The sound of Marissa's crying as she ran from him still rang in his ears and ached in his heart.

"Night Wolf?"

Brave Hawk called to him from outside the tepee and wrenched him from his troubled thoughts.

"*Gee-gee-kee-wayn-zee*, brother, I saw your return to the village, yet you did not come to me as promised," Brave Hawk said from beyond the walls of Night Wolf's lodge. "Can we talk now? I have much to ask you."

Knowing exactly what Brave Hawk wanted to say, Night Wolf wished he could deny his friend for a while longer. He still had no idea how to get around this situation. But he knew that the longer he put off the inevitable, the greater the chance that the tie between them might snap. He could not risk losing the camaraderie he had with Brave Hawk. It went back for too many years.

"Come on in, *gee-gee-kee-wayn-zee*," Night Wolf called, knowing that he had taken too long to respond to his friend. Never before in their relationship had there been a pause in response to one another. It had always been done with eagerness, with fondness.

Night Wolf's eyes wavered as Brave Hawk shoved the entrance flap aside and stopped to gaze quietly at him. In that one look, Night Wolf knew that his friend felt the strain between them. He was afraid that after today he and Brave Hawk might never be friends again.

"My brother, I see that you are still troubled by something," Brave Hawk said. "Should I come later?"

"No, no, please stay," Night Wolf said, gesturing toward Brave Hawk with a sweep of a hand. "*Mah-bee-szhon*, come. Sit beside me. We shall share a smoke and talk."

Brave Hawk smiled, let the entrance flap fall back in place to give them privacy, then sat down on a thick pallet of furs beside Night Wolf.

The fire's glow on Night Wolf's face made Brave Hawk uneasy. He realized that nothing about Night Wolf was the same. Something had changed since their last time together, when they had met at a council of many tribes. It troubled him that anything could come between them after having been so close.

Night Wolf rose and went to the back of his lodge to get his *ah-pwah-gun*, smoking pipe, which was wrapped neatly in buckskin. He carried it back to where Brave Hawk sat silently watching him, set it down, and sat cross-legged on the pelts. Slowly he unfolded the corners of the buckskin to reveal a red stone pipe. It had a long stem made from birch wood taken from a tree in the lake country of Minnesota.

This had been his father's pipe and his grandfather's before him. Night Wolf hoped to have a son to whom he could hand the pipe one day when he became a chief.

But now there might not be a son. The chief would be named from someone else's family. This pipe would leave his family. Night Wolf did not believe he would marry, for he would not marry without true, passionate love.

He laid the pipe across his lap. He reached for a tiny buckskin bundle and loosened its drawstrings. The aroma of dry willow bark tobacco wafted into the air as Night Wolf reached inside, took pinches of the tobacco between his fingers, and filled the bowl of the pipe.

He laid the small bag aside, pressed the tobacco more tightly into the bowl and with a stick from his lodge fire, lighted it.

After two puffs, he put the pipe down and raised his eyes and arms to the sky to invoke the Great Spirit, *Wenebojo*, imploring him to look with favor upon the conversation he was going to have with Brave Hawk.

Then he drew on the pipe two more times to

send the smoke as homage to *Wenebojo*, who could bring him and his friend joy or sadness, understanding or misunderstanding.

He handed the pipe to Brave Hawk and watched as he took two puffs, then handed it back. Night Wolf set the pipe on one of the rocks that surrounded his firepit.

"I find it hard to tell you what must be said. I hope that we will still be friends and allies," Night Wolf said, resting his hands on his knees.

"Say it, my brother, and do not fret. I cannot think of anything that might come between us," Brave Hawk said, replicating the sitting position of his friend. "Even if it is about my sister, I will understand."

"You have watched my silence and have read it well," Night Wolf said, sighing heavily, thankful for his friend's astuteness. He felt guilty for having doubted Brave Hawk's friendship. "I wanted to bring our families together through the bond of marriage but something has happened that will not allow it."

"Who is the *ee-quay*, woman?" Brave Hawk asked, searching Night Wolf's wavering eyes. "Yes, it is a woman who has changed things, my brother," Brave Hawk hurriedly went on. "Let me tell you something that might lift whatever guilt you might be feeling over this broken alliance. My sister is not innocent. Her heart also has wandered to someone else."

Night Wolf's eyes widened. He leaned forward. "Are you saying that she is in love with another man, that she does not wish to be my wife?"

"*Ay-uh*, though it was forbidden for him to love her, or she him," Brave Hawk said, folding his arms across his bare chest, his eyes on the flames of the fire now, instead of on Night Wolf.

"Was he white?" Night Wolf asked, drawing Brave Hawk's eyes. "Most people see love between two different colors as taboo. Did she fall in love with a *chee-mo-ko-man*, white man? Did she leave him behind in the land of the lakes?"

"He is white, and *ay-uh*, she left him behind," Brave Hawk said. "But his color is not the reason they did not marry."

"Why, then?" Night Wolf asked, his heart sinking. If Blue Star had been able to marry someone else, then his refusal of her would not create any heartache or embarrassment.

"He is a man who wears the black robe of the white man's God," Brave Hawk said tightly. "A man of the cloth cannot marry a woman."

Brave Hawk leaned closer to Night Wolf and

lowered his voice. "But, my brother, she does not know that I know so much about her relationship with this man. She never confided in me about him. It was the way they behaved when they were together. It was easy to see that they were in love. That sort of love is not so easily hidden."

"You are certain that she loved this man?" Night Wolf prodded.

"I know my sister well, almost as well as she knows herself. I know that she lost her heart to Father Scott Taylor and left it behind with him," Brave Hawk said. "She came to big sky country knowing that she would marry you, and she had accepted that. I even believe that after she saw you again she was happy to become your wife. Perhaps she saw in you a way to forget Father Taylor."

"And now I must turn my back on her," Night Wolf said.

"Then you plan to marry the woman you have lost your heart to?" Brave Hawk asked. "My sister will understand. She knows too well the ache of losing in love. She would not want you to lose as well."

Brave Hawk smiled and placed a hand on Night Wolf's shoulder. "I knew that you could not have changed your mind because you were disappointed after having seen her. What man would not want her? She is truly *mee-kah-wah-diz-ee*, beautiful."

"*Gah-ween*, no, it has nothing at all to do with your sister," Night Wolf assured him. "It is my stolen heart."

"Then when is the wedding ceremony?" Brave Hawk asked.

"There will be none," Night Wolf said. "It is not something that will ever happen."

"You are in love, yet you will not marry?" Brave Hawk leaned forward and looked directly into Night Wolf's eyes.

"No, there will be no marriage," Night Wolf said.

"Why?" Brave Hawk asked.

"Because this woman is fighting her feelings for me."

"Why is this?" Brave Hawk prodded.

"I am certain it has to do with her *gee-ba-ba*, father." Night Wolf remembered Marissa's father shouting at her to get away from Night Wolf, as though Night Wolf would soil his daughter.

"Her father does not want her to touch skin of my color, much less fall in love and marry me." Night Wolf's voice filled with anger.

"If you are not marrying this woman you say you love, then why can you not marry my sister?" Brave Hawk asked.

"Because I would do your sister a disservice. I can never love her as she deserves to be loved by a husband," Night Wolf replied. "Your sister deserves all the loyalty, all the love of a husband, not a man who dreams of another woman while sleeping with his wife."

Blue Star had arrived outside of Night Wolf's tepee in time to hear him say why he could not marry her. She did not have to hear Night Wolf speak Marissa's name to know that it was she to whom he referred.

She replayed the scene outside of the trading post in her mind. Marissa had humiliated Night Wolf, yet he still would turn his back on Blue Star? Although Blue Star loved someone else, she still planned to marry Night Wolf. She wanted to make him a good wife. And after seeing his handsomeness and knowing that he was a man with a good heart, she knew she could be happy with him.

In time, she had hoped, Father Scott Taylor would no longer be in her heart.

But now Night Wolf was not going to marry her. And because of a woman who had refused him.

Blue Star turned on her heel and rushed back to the corral, where she had left the palomino pony. She led it out, making sure it did not make any disturbance that would alert

Chapter 18

Marissa sat beside her bedroom window and looked out with longing for a moment. She tried to concentrate on the sweater she was knitting for her father.

Her fingers trembled, causing her to have trouble controlling the needles, and they slid together clumsily, making her drop a stitch. She yanked at the yarn and corrected her error.

Night Wolf.

How could she have actually run away from him like she did after they had shared such a wonderful, passionate kiss?

"Oh, what must he think of me now?" she whispered, dropping another stitch. She slammed the needles and the knitting down on the table beside her chair.

She buried her face in her hands as she tried to remember Father Mulvaney's warnings. She must forget Night Wolf. He was promised to another woman. And their attraction had already created tension between her father and the Cree community. Her father's success at his newly established trading post depended on her and how she behaved.

She had a strange sort of ache in the pit of her stomach. She wanted to go to Night Wolf and beg his forgiveness over her reaction to his kiss. He probably thought that she had disliked it.

She rose from the chair and stood at the window, then found herself gazing in the direction of the Cree village. It would not take all that long to get there, and if she left now, she could return home before nightfall.

"What am I thinking?" she whispered, whirling around and pacing the floor.

She slowly ran her fingers across her lips, reliving the kiss, tasting and smelling him. And how blissful it had been to have had her breasts crushed against his powerful chest. Never had anything been as heavenly as that.

"Please stop this!" she said aloud, then looked quickly at the door, hoping that her father had not heard.

This was the time of day when he took a nap. Until trading began in the spring, he was able to pamper himself with daily naps.

A sudden excitement blossomed within her. She looked toward the window again. The sun was only halfway down from the midpoint of the sky.

A wave of guilt overcame her at the thought of betraying her father's trust.

"But I must," she said, now determined to go to the Cree village and apologize to Night Wolf. She did not want him to think that she found his kiss and embrace unsavory, when it was just the opposite. She wanted him to think kindly of her when he saw her, or thought of her, even if he was married to another woman.

It was just not their destiny to be together.

Once at the village she would make whatever peace she could with Night Wolf, and then delve into the secret that had been guarded so well through the years by her father.

She knelt in front of her trunk, eager to get dressed for the ride. The lid was open, and her clothes were laid absently over its edges. She chose a brown leather riding skirt that was soft as butter to the touch and a long-sleeved white blouse, then reached beneath her bed for her riding boots.

Her mother had always scolded her for not being as tidy as she had been taught to be. It hurt too much to think about her.

But now she might be able to find her birth mother. She would go to the Cree village and

seek out answers that only one person had—
the person who had given birth to her.

After she dressed, Marissa went to the table
beside her bed and opened the drawer. Her father insisted that she keep the small pearl-
handled pistol close in case someone tried to
accost her in the darkness while she slept.

She realized she should be more careful riding alone and knew her father would want her
to carry the pistol. Now she lifted the pistol
from the drawer, checked to see if it had bullets
in its chamber. When she saw that it was fully
loaded, she slid it into the pocket of her skirt
and walked purposefully toward her door.

Slowly she opened it and stepped cautiously
out into the corridor. She paused to look at her
father's closed bedroom door, then smiled at
the sound of his rumbling snores.

"The necklace—" she whispered.

She hurried back to her dressing table and
got the necklace.

She gazed at it for a moment as it lay in her
hand. She tried to envision how small she had
been for that tiny thing to fit around her neck.

The thought renewed her determination to
find the mother who had placed it there.

She slid the necklace into the pocket opposite
the gun.

She left the cabin, readied her horse, then led

it into the forest, knowing that its hoofbeats would be muffled by the autumn leaves which cushioned the ground.

She glanced quickly over at the mission and again remembered the warnings of Father Mulvaney. Repent. Forget the Cree chief.

She mounted and rode at a lope beneath the trees until she came alongside the river. The shine of the water reflected the sun into her eyes as she thought about her future.

Chapter 19

Blue Star rode close to the river, and stayed in the shadows of the tall, yellow-leafed aspens in case someone came along.

She was not going to harm Marissa, only put fear into her heart. This fear had to be so deeply embedded that she would be afraid to tell anyone of Blue Star's threats.

It was not Blue Star's usual behavior to threaten anyone, but she had to do what she could to ensure her marriage to Night Wolf.

He would make a wonderful husband, and she wanted him for her own. She knew that as long as Marissa was in love with Night Wolf, there was a chance she might change her mind and go to him and say that she was ready to marry him. Night Wolf would never change his mind and marry Blue Star as long as this was a possibility. He had to know for certain that Marissa was no longer available.

The white woman must be removed from

Night Wolf's mind and his life in order for a change of heart to take place. Blue Star was ready to take the first step required for that change.

The golden leaves above her rustled in the breeze, making a sound like falling rain.

Blue Star smiled when she heard the squawk of a blue jay. It reminded her of her home in Minnesota, where blue jays were thick in the trees every autumn, fussing as though they knew the cold winds of winter would soon make their existence hard.

She wondered just how cold it got in this country. Minnesota winters were cold and snow-filled. She could not deny being excited about the prospects of living in a new land and learning everything she could about it.

Her thoughts were stilled as she drew a tight rein. A uniformed man on a lovely white mustang blocked her path. Blue Star's palomino came to a shuddering halt. It whinnied loudly and shook its thick mane.

"What do you want of me?" Blue Star asked the man. She ran a hand down her pony's neck in an effort to calm it. "Why do you stop me?"

The blue-uniformed soldier's lips lifted into a quivering, slow smile, displaying a chipped front tooth. He seemed to be mentally undressing her as he looked slowly up and down the length of her. The man made her skin crawl and her insides grow cold.

Blue Star had been told to show courage in the face of danger. "Move," she said, tightening her jaw and boldly lifting her chin. "Let me pass. I am on a mission."

"A mission, eh?" Bradley Coomer said, chuckling. His eyes bored into hers sharply. "What sort?"

"It has nothing to do with you, so you do not need to know anything about it," Blue Star said, tensing when he edged his horse close to hers.

"Nothing to do with me?" Bradley repeated his eyes gleaming. "Well, let's see about that. Let's *make* it my business."

"What do you mean?" Blue Star said, flinching when he began slowly circling her horse with his.

"You'll see," he sneered.

As he circled behind her pony, she saw her chance to get away from him. The mission was not far. She would seek help there. The black-robed men were surely as kind and protective as Father Scott Taylor.

She flicked her reins, kicked her moccasined heels against the pony's flanks, and lay low over its back as she galloped away from the soldier.

Her heart raced, and she was flooded with emotion all born of terror, as the man made chase. The thundering hoofbeats told her that he was gaining on her. Then he was there, at her side, smiling that evil smile. He grabbed her reins and drew her horse up short.

Strangely enough, he handed her reins back to her, then tauntingly began circling her horse with his once more. "You remind me of another redskin girl. The one who gave me this," Bradley smiled, showing his chipped tooth. "She was a feisty one. Took a rock to me. Didn't stop me, though."

Blue Star was breathless with fear, yet reached deep inside herself for the courage that had been instilled by her father.

Again she snapped her reins, kicked her pony, and rode off as hard as she could in the direction of the mission.

This time, when he reached her and grabbed her reins she could see the hate in his eyes. She knew her chance to escape had just passed her by.

"You can run, but I'll catch you," he said with a bitter laugh. "I always do."

He was enjoying this game of his. He

laughed throatily as he once again handed her reins to her and allowed her to ride away.

Blue Star knew that each time he allowed her a few moments of freedom, she got closer to the mission. Just a little farther and she could get rid of this man. Yet she knew that he would not allow her to go much farther without finishing what he had started.

The thought of rape made her throat constrict, but she fought the urge to vomit, and continued to ride hard through the forest.

She still hoped that she might outsmart the soldier and make it to the mission.

Tears filled her eyes and her fear got the best of her. She became momentarily blinded by the tears and rode into a low-hanging branch, which knocked her off her horse.

As she landed on the ground, her ankle twisted, and the wind was knocked out of her. She was aware of blood streaming down the front of her face, and of the excruciating pain in her head and ankle.

Through the blood and tears, she saw the white man ride up next to her. She brushed her face clean with her trembling fingers and saw him staring down at her from his saddle.

He laughed mockingly, but just as he started to dismount, he stopped and jerked his head around. Alarm lighted his eyes at the sound of a horse.

Hope surged into Blue Star's heart. Someone was going to find this man amid his act of madness. She scarcely breathed as she awaited his response.

He glared down at her again, then rode quickly away in the opposite direction from the other horse.

Desperate to get away, Blue Star tried to stand, but fell back to the ground. Her sprained ankle wouldn't hold her full weight. She couldn't walk. She was trapped. She looked frantically around for her horse but didn't see it anywhere.

Whoever had been riding a short distance away had gone on, unaware that someone needed help.

Panic seized her at the thought of the white man returning.

Sobbing, she started to crawl but when she had gone only a short distance, she stopped, exhausted.

She needed to hide.

She crawled as close to a tree as possible and reached around her for dead, fallen leaves. She covered herself, then waited, hoping that someone she knew would come and rescue her. She now wished that she had not left the village without telling someone, yet had she told, they would have known what she had planned for the white woman.

She had made a trap for herself, and now she must find a way to cope with it, alone.

Aware of the throbbing of her head, Blue Star fought against unconsciousness, but she felt herself drifting off into a dull black void.

Chapter 20

Marissa had stopped beside the river to think about her decision to see Night Wolf.

It was a brisk, windy day, and she watched the fallen yellow aspen leaves float by in the river, their edges curled and looking like miniature canoes. Tiny minnows darted around beneath the surface of the water, taking advantage of the sun. She felt the coolness of the day and wished that she had brought a shawl to wrap around her shoulders.

But most of all, she felt torn again.

She looked toward her home. She wondered if she should return there and talk all this over with her father. Then she gazed in the direction of the Cree village. She was filled with such longing. She wanted to know her mother, but she needed a man for the first time in her life.

If she went to the village, wouldn't it make her ache for Night Wolf even worse?

Yet, the only way she would ever be able to search out the truth of her real mother would be to go there.

She had to remember Night Wolf's promise to Blue Star. But if he loved Blue Star, why had he kissed Marissa?

"Oh, this is so hard," she whispered as she raked her fingers through her long black tresses.

She knew that she must return home. She must talk with her father and make him understand her desire to know her true mother. She wanted his permission, his blessing, to go to the Cree village. She would promise him that she would not see or speak with Night Wolf. Her visit would have only one purpose. To find her mother.

Sighing, she mounted her horse and wheeled it back around in the direction of her home. She rode slowly alongside the river, but stopped when she saw movement. She leaned to her right, her eyes slowly searching the dark shadows of the aspens.

Then she saw it.

A beautiful palomino pony was moving slowly through the forest. Its saddle was empty. Whoever had been riding this lovely pony must have been thrown. The rider might be lying somewhere close by, injured.

Dismounting quickly, Marissa walked toward the pony to take its reins. But her approach alarmed it and it broke into a hard gallop and disappeared into the shadows of the forest.

Marissa went back to her own horse, took its reins, then walked slowly along the edges of the forest. Her eyes looked guardedly into the deep shadows, then up ahead, then behind her. She suddenly felt in danger herself.

It was best to hurry on to the protection of her home. She would tell her father about the pony, and its missing rider. He would know what to do. He would go to the fort and tell the officer there and the colonel could send out soldiers to scout the area.

Just as she started to mount, she heard someone sobbing. She couldn't go home without finding the person. She could not abandon whoever it was. She would not be a coward and leave.

Her shoulders squared, her jaw tight, she tied her reins to the tree limb, then slowly walked ahead, searching in earnest. Her eyes moved from place to place, and she kept her hand in her pocket, her fingers curled around her tiny pistol.

If anyone threatened her, she would not hesitate to fire the pistol.

Not seeing signs of anyone, she dared to call out, hoping that the wrong person would not hear her. She was aware of the sudden silence. Whoever was there was too afraid to allow anyone to know where they were. Not even a woman.

She took her pistol from the pocket and held it out before her. The victim might not be alone, after all, but with some sinister character who had harmed her. Marissa was certain that it was a woman whose cries she had heard. There was no mistaking a woman's sobs.

Growing more afraid that this could be a trap to lure her farther into the darkness of the forest, Marissa held her firearm steady before her, and kept a finger on the trigger.

She again called for whoever was there to speak up.

When no one responded, Marissa explained that she was a friend and that she was there to offer help. She asked if the person was alone.

Still getting no response, and no longer hearing the sobs, Marissa walked stealthily onward.

She half stumbled over a pile of leaves and looked quickly down at them. She gasped when she saw dark, frightened eyes peering out from the leaves. Stunned, she took a step away. A hand brushed the leaves entirely from the face.

Marissa quickly lowered the gun to her side when she saw that it was none other than Blue Star!

Chapter 21

Marissa slid the pistol into her skirt pocket, then fell to her knees and hurriedly uncovered Blue Star.

She gasped when she saw her bloody brow. Blue Star winced as Marissa reached down and touched her right ankle.

"How did this happen?" Marissa blurted out. "Did you fall from your horse? Why did you cover yourself?"

Marissa felt the color drain from her face and looked furtively around her. Blue Star would have covered herself with leaves only because she was frightened and was trying to hide from someone.

She looked back down at Blue Star. Her ankle was obviously swollen, no doubt sprained. She couldn't walk.

"Blue Star, please answer me," Marissa said, aware of Blue Star staring at her defiantly. She refused to answer Marissa, even though they could be in danger if the person who had done this to Blue Star was somewhere near.

"I am here to help you," Marissa soothed. She reached to flick a piece of dried leaf from Blue Star's cheek but flinched and drew her hand quickly back when Blue Star's stare turned venomous and she tried to scoot farther away from Marissa.

"I do not want your help," Blue Star said. "You have taken away my future—my man. There is to be no wedding between me and Night Wolf, and it is because of you. Leave!"

Marissa was speechless. There wasn't going to be a wedding. She now understood the sudden change in Blue Star's attitude toward her.

Had Night Wolf told Blue Star that he loved Marissa?

Father Mulvaney's words and her father's orders came to Marissa's mind, reminding her just how impossible it was to think there could be a future for her with Night Wolf.

But if he wasn't going to marry Blue Star?

She had resigned herself to stepping away from him and never loving him again. She had been ready to try to get a new start in her life, perhaps find another man. There were many bachelors at Fort Harris. Surely among them was someone she could love . . .

"You just stand there?" Blue Star said, her

eyes flashing with anger. "Leave me. Leave me now. I can find my own way back home."

Marissa watched as Blue Star tried to get up, then fell back down when her ankle gave out.

"You know that you are in no condition to go anywhere. Why else would you have been hiding beneath a pile of leaves?" Marissa said.

She raised an eyebrow. "Why did you hide in such a way?" she asked. "Did someone cause this?"

Realizing that she had no choice now but to accept Marissa's help, and afraid that the red-haired man might return at any moment, Blue Star relented.

"A man came and taunted me while I was on my pony," she said, her voice breaking. "He circled my steed, laughing and looking at me. When I tried to ride away from him, he followed and stopped me."

She swallowed hard, then continued. "A second time I got away, but only because he allowed me to. When he bragged about having accosted another woman of my skin color, I became so afraid I began crying. My tears blinded me, and I did not see a low limb. I ran into it."

When Blue Star stopped to wipe the tears from her eyes and find the courage to continue, Marissa wanted to reach out and pull her into her arms, to comfort her. But she knew that she couldn't do that. She was lucky that Blue Star had opened up to her at all.

"The man heard a horse and was afraid of getting caught, so he rode away," Blue Star said. "But no one came on a horse. Whoever it was went elsewhere. I was afraid the evil man would return, so I tried to crawl to where I could hide. My ankle hurt me so much, I could not get far. I covered myself with leaves."

"So the palomino pony that I saw was yours," Marissa said, looking over her shoulder at her own horse.

"Yes, but it is not mine. It is Night Wolf's," Blue Star murmured.

Blue Star looked around her. "Where is Night Wolf's steed? I want to go home."

"You are too far from your home to get there while you are in such a condition," Marissa said. "And it is not safe for you to travel while that man might be somewhere near."

"Night Wolf's steed," Blue Star insisted stubbornly. "Where is it? I wish to return home."

"It ran off," Marissa said. "Please understand that you are in no condition to travel far. And it is *not* safe. I can tell that you had quite a blow to your head. And your ankle. It won't even hold you. Let me take you to the mission. It's only a short distance from here. There is a priest there who was a physician before he entered into the priesthood. Let him doctor your wounds. You should rest while I go and report what happened to you."

Listening to Marissa speak of priests made Blue Star's heart ache. She could not help but think of Father Scott Taylor. If she went to the mission, she would again feel his loss so vividly.

Yet she knew that the longer. she and Marissa stayed in the forest alone, the better were the chances of her assailant returning. She hoped never to see that man again.

"Yes, take me to the mission," Blue Star said. "I know of priests and the good they do. I will feel comfortable with them."

"I'm glad. I truly believe that we are not safe here," Marissa said. She pushed herself up from the ground. "I shall go for my horse. We will travel together to the mission."

She started to walk away, then gazed down at Blue Star again. "Can you describe who did this to you?"

"There was such a cruel coldness in his blue eyes as he taunted me," Blue Star said, pushing herself up to a sitting position. Then she grabbed at her head and swayed slightly, as though she might faint.

"He had hair the color of a red sunset," Blue

Star continued. "His face was not smooth. He wore a blue uniform—and I remember one of his front teeth had a chip in it. He bragged to me that—that—he accosted another Indian woman and she used a rock to fend him off. He called her a feisty one."

Marissa gasped. Blue Star had described Bradley Coomer. She shuddered at the thought that he could be this cruel. She suddenly felt threatened herself.

"I suddenly feel ill to my stomach," Blur Star said, clutching at her belly. "I feel faint. My head. It throbs so. Please . . . hurry. Please . . ."

Marissa ran to her horse and grabbed its reins, then led it back to Blue Star, who now lay on the ground, her eyes closed.

She knelt at her side. "Blue Star, are you conscious?" she asked, gently touching her arm.

Blue Star weakly opened her eyes and nodded.

"You have to help me get you on my horse," Marissa said, carefully taking Blue Star by an arm and urging her to her feet. "Lift the one foot. There is no need to put your weight on it. And put an arm around my shoulder. I shall manage to get you on the horse. But help however you can."

Blue Star nodded again, though she felt ready to drift off into a dark void. "Hurry," she whispered, her voice anxious. "I am not certain how long I can stay awake. My head. Oh, my head!"

"I know," Marissa said, placing an arm around Blue Star's waist. "But you must fight against blacking out, even after you are on the horse. I'm afraid I wouldn't be able to hold you there and ride the horse at the same time."

"I . . . shall . . . try," Blue Star said, her voice breaking.

Finally Blue Star was on the horse, and Marissa mounted in front her.

"Blue Star, you *must* fight to stay awake," Marissa ordered as she looked over her shoulder at the injured Chippewa woman. "Can you stay awake a while longer? We aren't that far from the mission."

"I will stay awake," Blue Star said, yet she felt more light-headed than earlier. Blue Star placed her arms around Marissa's waist and clung to her. "But hurry."

"I can't ride at a hard gallop or you might fall off," Marissa said, flicking her reins, moving at a slow lope.

Marissa thought again about Bradley Coomer. Her jaw tightened and her eyes flashed angrily. It sickened her to think that her father might have married her off to that red-headed beast, and then she would have been the wife of a man whose heart was as evil as it was cold.

The only good thing to come out of what had happened today was that she knew that Night Wolf had changed his mind about marrying Blue Star. That meant that he was a free man, to love as he wished to love, to marry whom he wished to marry.

Now if Marissa could feel as free.

Chapter 22

Marissa was glad to have finally reached the mission, but she felt the color drain from her face when her father stepped outside. Their eyes met and locked.

She could scarcely breathe as her father's gaze jerked to Blue Star, who still clung to Marissa's waist.

Now Marissa had something else to fear. Her father. He had obviously awakened and found her gone. He had more than likely checked the mission to see if she was there and discovered that she wasn't. Now his missing daughter was arriving with an Indian woman.

"Father, please help me," Marissa pleaded. "We can talk about things after we get Blue Star inside the mission."

Marissa looked past her father just as Father Mulvaney came outside, stopping quickly when he saw the women on the horse. He rushed to them, and just as he reached up for Blue Star, she fainted and fell into his arms.

"What happened to her?" Father Mulvaney asked as he held her.

"Yes, what happened to her, and why on earth are you with her?" Joseph asked, coming quickly to take Blue Star from Father Mulvaney's arms. The elderly priest's back was bending with the strain of holding the woman.

"Father, I'll explain later," Marissa said, looking nervously over her shoulder. She felt blessed to have reached the mission without Bradley ambushing them. She looked at the fort and felt a bitterness in the depths of her throat. The thought of that man ever touching her made her feel physically ill.

"Marissa, answer me," Joseph demanded, still standing there holding Blue Star, not seeming to know what he should do with her.

Marissa looked down at her father, then dismounted. She nervously twisted the reins around her fingers as she stood in the path of her father's scowl.

"Please take her inside and then I will explain," she said. "I have so much to tell you, Father, but first, let's see to Blue Star."

Father Mulvaney touched Joseph gently on an arm.

"Come with me," he said, ignoring Joseph's

scowl. "The woman has fainted. Her head is bloody and by the way her ankle is swollen, it is either broken or sprained."

"Sprained," Marissa quickly interjected.

"Thank the good Lord for that," Father Mulvaney said, nodding toward Joseph. "Follow me. We can take Blue Star to a room that is used for overnight visitors. It's at the back of the chapel. It is comfortable and warm, with its own fireplace. Father Jamieson was a physician before he entered the priesthood. He will see to her injuries."

Joseph frowned at Marissa again, then followed Father Mulvaney into the mission and to a small room. Several dried pinecones lay in a basket beside the fireplace. Not only could they be used to heat the room, but they gave it a pleasant fragrance as well.

Marissa saw a bed with a pretty patchwork quilt thrown across it. On one side of it stood a table with a kerosene lamp on it. On the other side was a wooden chair.

The hardwood floor had a braided rug covering most of the surface. Along one wall stood the stone fireplace, cold ashes on the hearth.

"I shall light the lantern and get a warm fire going," she said as her father carefully placed Blue Star on the bed.

Father Mulvaney looked from Marissa to her father, almost afraid to leave them alone, but he had to think of Blue Star first. He hurriedly left the room to get Father Jamieson.

Marissa was aware of her father's glare even though her back was to him. She placed wood on the grate, along with several of the pinecones. She tried not to think of the berating she would soon be getting. She hoped that her father would at least wait until later, when they were in the privacy of their home.

Soon flames were lapping around the logs and the pinecones were aglow with fire.

"Marissa, I want answers," Joseph said as she stood and turned slowly toward him. "Now. Before Father Mulvaney arrives with Father Jamieson. When I awakened from my nap, I found you gone. I did not check the livery stable because I thought that you respected my wishes enough not to . . . well. . . . I came to see if you were with Father Mulvaney. When I discovered that you weren't, I knew where you must be. Marissa, were you going to the Cree village to see Night Wolf, or to see if you could discover who your true mother was?"

"Father, is any of that important now?" Marissa asked. "This young woman is injured. Don't you care at all about that? It's not like you to be so insensitive to the needs of others.

She was accosted, Father. Ambushed. Blue Star is unconscious."

"Hold on," Joseph said, waving a hand in the air. "You are going too fast for me. Start from the beginning, Marissa. Tell me why you left. Then tell me how you happen to be with the Indian woman."

Neither of them had a chance to say anything else, for Father Mulvaney came into the room with Father Jamieson. The priest looked about forty years of age, handsome, yet in a frail sort of way. His face was colorless, as though he avoided being in the sun. His dark eyes were a contrast against the white of his skin, and his golden hair was tied in a ponytail that hung down to his waist.

She watched Father Jamieson bend over and examine Blue Star. He looked at Marissa. "Tell me how she was injured," he said, then turned to Father Mulvaney. "Please see to it that I get a warm basin of water and clean cloths. And she will need a warm, nourishing bowl of soup later."

Father Mulvaney nodded, then left the room. Father Jamieson sat down in the chair to await his return.

Joseph said, "Now, tell us exactly how you found her. We'll get into the whys of things when we are alone."

"Yes, sir," Marissa gulped out. "I understand."

She went and knelt on the floor beside the bed and took one of Blue Star's hands in hers, as the pretty woman slept.

In her mind's eye she recalled the hate in Blue Star's eyes when Marissa found her beneath the leaves. She would never forget the venomous way Blue Star spoke to her, even though she should have been grateful that it was Marissa, not Bradley Coomer, who found her.

"Father, when I tell you who is responsible, you won't want to believe it," Marissa blurted out. "Father, it was Bradley Coomer. He ambushed Blue Star. He taunted her over and over again. All along planning . . . planning . . ."

She stopped and looked away from her father to Father Jamieson. His blue eyes were wide and filled with disbelief.

"Father Jamieson, there *are* evil men on this earth, and one of them wears the uniform of our United States cavalry," Marissa said.

She turned to her father again. "Bradley led Blue Star to believe he was allowing her to leave. She rode hard away from him. But . . . but . . . she was crying and her tears blinded her, so she didn't see a low-hanging tree limb and ran straight into it. That was how she injured her forehead. She was thrown from her horse and injured her ankle."

Her father's face drained of color as Marissa continued to describe the assailant as Blue Star had. Anyone who knew Bradley Coomer would know that the description fit him perfectly.

Father Mulvaney came into the room with a basin of water and towels. He had a robe draped over an arm. Talk of Bradley was halted.

"Marissa, I have brought a robe for the woman," Father Mulvaney said, handing it to her. "I've also brought the basin of water and cloths. Would you mind removing her bloody clothes and bathing her? Father Jamieson will do the rest when you are through."

"Yes, I'll be glad to do whatever I can to help Blue Star," Marissa said. She gave her father a quick glance. "Father, before you do anything, please wait. I want to discuss it further with you."

"But you said it was Bradley," he said, his eyes filled with anger.

"Yes, but please wait. Let me get Blue Star cleansed and comfortable, then while Father Jamieson is treating her wounds, we can talk."

"Let us go into the chapel," Father Mulvaney said, nodding to both Father Jamieson and Joseph. "Joseph, give your daughter time to do what must be done. Then we can do what we can for the injured woman."

Joseph gave Marissa a look over his shoulder as he left with the two priests. Marissa cringed as she pulled the bloody dress gently over Blue Star's head.

As she bathed Blue Star, she kept glancing at her to see if she was regaining consciousness. But she slept soundly, her breathing thankfully even. Marissa hoped that she would soon awaken, proving that she was going to be all right.

After the white cotton gown was on Blue Star, and the patchwork blanket covered her up to her armpits, Marissa stood up and hurried to the chapel.

"You can go in now," she said, looking from Father Mulvaney to Father Jamieson. "Please help her. She looks so . . . so . . . innocent in her sleep, so helpless."

"We will do what we can," Father Mulvaney said, placing a gentle hand on Father Jamieson's arm. The two men left the chapel.

Marissa turned to her father and smiled weakly at him. "I know," she murmured. "I'm ready for that lecture."

Joseph took Marissa by a hand and led her outside for some privacy. He took both her hands in his. His eyes wavered as he gazed into hers.

"Daughter, I regret more and more returning to the land of your heritage," he said, his voice drawn. "Things are getting way too complicated. This Indian woman you rescued today will be indebted to you. Aren't you tempted to ask her to help you find some answers? Wasn't that why you had left? You were on your way to the Cree village when you found the injured Indian lady."

"Yes, I do want answers," Marissa said. "I was on my way to the Cree village even though I was going against your wishes. But, Father, this is my life. I am an adult. I deserve to know everything about me. Why can't you understand that?"

"Daughter, your mother and I left this country for the sole purpose of keeping you from ever discovering the truth about your heritage," Joseph said. "We didn't want you ever to find out."

"Yet you came back to my roots," Marissa said, searching his eyes. "Why would you chance bringing me back here? Didn't you consider the possibility that I would discover the truth? Didn't you think that I might discover that my life up until now was a lie?"

"No, I didn't consider it for one minute,"

Joseph said, releasing her hands. He clasped his behind him. "I thought that enough years had passed. You are grown. You were a mere baby then."

"Father, I still wouldn't know had you not told that—that—rogue Bradley Coomer," Marissa said tightly. "Of all people, Bradley? You had to be desperate to want me married to that cad. You knew that I would discover the truth. You surely knew that Bradley would tell me."

"Had he loved you like I wanted him to love you, he would have respected you too much to do anything that might cause you harm," Joseph said, balling his hands into fists at his sides. "How wrong I was. How stupid I was not to see right through that man and know that he was not worthy of being your husband."

"But you didn't, nor has Colonel James. He took him in and made him his protégé," Marissa said, visibly shivering. "The thought of that man getting near me makes me want to vomit. If he hadn't heard a horse approaching, he would have raped Blue Star. That was the man you wanted me to sleep next to every night?"

"I was wrong," Joseph choked out.

"Father, think about it," Marissa said. "Had

he succeeded at raping her, perhaps even killing her, he could have caused an Indian uprising. He must be punished. He must be thrown out of the cavalry, even imprisoned. He must be dealt with quickly to prove to the Indians that men like him do not go unpunished."

"You are certain that it was he?" Joseph asked, looking over his shoulder at the fort, then into Marissa's eyes again. "Couldn't it possibly have been someone who looked like him?"

"Father, surely two men would not have the same chip in the tooth," Marissa said. "It was Bradley. I have no doubt about it."

She quickly told him about Bradley's earlier confrontation with an Indian maiden and how she had defended herself by hitting him in the face with a rock.

"I abhor the very thought of such evil acts, especially since I was so adamant that he marry you," her father said grimly. His jaw tightened, and his eyes narrowed. "I will take care of this, but promise that you will never leave alone again."

He put his hands on her shoulders. "Daughter, do not tempt fate."

Her eyes wavered. She couldn't promise him anything. He knew that she would not promise him something, then do otherwise. She had to find answers, and she couldn't find them by hiding away in their home.

Joseph realized that he was wasting his breath by insisting that she do as he asked. He decided then and there to take Marissa away—and soon, before the river froze over. He would find a buyer later for his trading post. The important thing was to get Marissa back to Kansas.

"Marissa, Blue Star is awake now," Father Mulvaney said, interrupting the strained conversation between her and her father.

Marissa turned to look at the priest. "Is she all right?" she asked, already walking toward him.

"Well enough to eat a bowl of soup," Father Mulvaney said as he took Marissa's hand and walked into the mission with her. "Father Jamieson saw to her wounds and is now feeding her. There seems to be a connection between the two. They seem to have become instant friends."

"Truly?" Marissa said, raising her eyebrows. "Well, good for Father Jamieson, for I doubt that Blue Star will ever want to be my friend."

"After what you did for her?" Father Mulvaney said, stopping Marissa. She turned to face him. "You saved her life, Marissa. She won't ever forget that."

"Did she say that?" Marissa asked softly. "Does she consider what I did as saving her life?"

"If you had not come along when you did, who is to say what would have happened to her?" Father Mulvaney said, smiling warmly at Marissa.

"Goodness' sake, I only now realize that someone should go to the Cree village to tell them where Blue Star is and that she is all right," Marissa blurted out.

She glanced at the door. She knew that her father would die if she took on the chore. But the priests did not ride and she was not about to go to the fort to ask anyone there to do the deed. They would be learning about Bradley soon enough.

While her father was at the fort, she could leave. She had to do this for Blue Star. She wanted to prove that she was her friend.

Marissa did not feel threatened by going to the Indian village alone. Her only threat was her father's reaction, and she would deal with that when she had to. For now, all she would concern herself with was telling Night Wolf where Blue Star was, and that she was safe.

"Father Mulvaney, I can talk with Blue Star

later," Marissa said, anxious to leave. "But now I am going to the Cree village to tell them what has happened so that someone can come for her and take her home."

She smiled at Father Mulvaney. "Will you tell her that I am doing this for her?" she asked softly.

"I most certainly will," Father Mulvaney said, returning her smile. Then he frowned. "You know that you shouldn't be doing this. Your father is already quite angry at you for having gone against his wishes."

"But don't you see?" Marissa said. "If I don't go to tell them, who will?"

"I'll explain to your father," Father Mulvaney said, patting her head. "Go. But be careful. Watch out on all sides of you."

"The only one I have to fear will soon be taken care of," Marissa said. "After Father tells Colonel James about Bradley, his days of freedom will be over. He'll be locked away."

"What if Colonel James doesn't believe his protégé is capable of such sinful acts?" Father Mulvaney asked.

Marissa felt a rush of coldness around her heart. Perhaps no one *would* believe that Bradley could do such a heinous thing!

"Surely they will believe the truth when they hear it. Even Colonel James," Marissa said. She quickly hugged Father Mulvaney, then stepped away from him.

"Please tell Father where I am, and please make him see reason?" she pleaded.

"I shall try," Father Mulvaney said, nodding. "Godspeed, Marissa. Godspeed."

She swallowed hard, smiled, then unwound her horse's reins from the hitching rail. As she mounted, she glanced toward the fort.

The gate was open. Perhaps her father was even now telling the vicious truth about Bradley Coomer and what he was capable of.

"Please, Lord, please make them understand this man's evil heart and make him pay for his evil deeds," she prayed to herself.

Marissa rode off at a hard gallop toward the Indian village. She reached down and felt the security of her pistol in her front pocket. If Bradley did become a problem, she was ready for him.

Chapter 23

The fire's glow made dancing shadows along the inside walls of Night Wolf's tepee. Night Wolf was aware of the strain between himself and Brave Hawk as they sat together before the firepit. He regretted this. He and Brave Hawk had been friends for too long to allow anything to come between them.

"I am sorry about my decision not to marry Blue Star, but I know that it is best for her," Night Wolf said, leaning forward to lift a log into the flames.

"Your decision is honorable enough," Brave Hawk said, pulling a blanket more snugly around his muscled shoulders. "Had you married her without loving her, she would be filled with more pain than she is now."

"I do not anticipate ever marrying," Night Wolf said, his voice drawn. "I will not marry without love."

"Again, tell me why you cannot marry the

white woman?" Brave Hawk asked, gazing intensely at Night Wolf.

"I know that she has feelings for me," Night Wolf said. He sighed. "I saw it in her eyes when she looked at me. I felt it in the way she kissed me. She is fighting her feelings."

"You kissed her?" Brave Hawk said, his eyes widening.

"*Ay-uh*, I kissed her. She kissed me back," Night Wolf said solemnly. "But I was wrong to."

"Perhaps, in time, things will change so that you *can* marry the woman," Brave Hawk said softly. "I hope that in time I will find someone to share my life with. As it is, no one has caused my heart to beat faster. Nor have I seen a woman in my midnight dreams."

"Perhaps you will find someone among my tribe who pleases you," Night Wolf said. Immediately, he thought of his own sister and how she no longer had a husband. She was entrancingly beautiful. He wanted to suggest his sister to Brave Hawk now, but thought better of it.

"*Ay-uh*, it would be good to find someone with whom I could share my blankets every night. Someone who could give me children," Brave Hawk said.

He glanced toward the closed entrance flap.

Then he looked at Night Wolf again. "I gather Blue Star has gone to sit by the river. She did that often back at our village. She seeks solace often. I am certain that by the time I return to our tepee, she will be there preparing food for herself and me."

"She is a good cook?" Night Wolf asked.

"You will never know the wonder of all of my sister's skills by not marrying her," Brave Hawk said. "Perhaps another man will."

"She will find a man who will make her happy," Night Wolf replied.

"*Ay-uh*, she will. A woman as lovely as she should never be alone," Brave Hawk said, rising. "I must leave you now. Speaking of my sister's cooking has made me aware of the hunger in my belly."

Night Wolf smiled and rose to his feet and stepped outside with Brave Hawk. "Come soon, brother, and talk again," he said, placing a hand on Brave Hawk's muscled shoulder. "It is good to have these times with you. I look forward to the spring buffalo hunt. With you at my side, the pleasure will be twofold."

Brave Hawk seemed not to hear what he was saying. He stared at his recently erected tepee, which sat not far from Night Wolf's.

Brave Hawk's brow furrowed when he saw no smoke spiraling from the smoke hole. "My sister is not there," he said. "If she was, she would have our lodge fire burning. There is no smoke."

"Did she usually stay long by the river in many lake country?" Night Wolf asked, stepping over to look down at the river. He saw only the many canoes beached along the riverbank.

"I do not see anyone at the river," Brave Hawk said, joining him.

"Then where is she?" Night Wolf asked, a fear building in his heart to think that something might have happened to Blue Star.

"If she heard us talking earlier about my decision not to marry her . . ." Night Wolf began.

"Do you think that she did?" Brave Hawk asked, his voice drawn.

"Perhaps," Night Wolf said.

"I do not know how long she has been gone. She could have left hours ago," Brave Hawk said, nervously kneading his brow. "Night Wolf, I fear—"

Suddenly they heard the approach of a horse. They exchanged quick looks, then smiled.

"She went horseback riding," Brave Hawk said. "She is returning now."

They turned just as the palomino pony came into the village and stopped next to Night

Wolf. Alarm rushed through him when he saw that the saddle was empty.

Night Wolf grabbed the pony's reins. His breath caught in his throat as he noticed the blood on the pony's body and the saddle.

"My sister has been injured somehow," Brave Hawk exclaimed.

"Someone was injured, but we are not certain it was Blue Star," Night Wolf said. He hurriedly took the pony behind his tepee and led it into the corral with the other horses.

He didn't take the time to remove the saddle, but instead went with Brave Hawk to the center of the village. Night Wolf shouted for everyone to come and hear what he had to say. Soon all the people, Cree and Chippewa alike, were standing in a wide circle around Night Wolf and Brave Hawk, their eyes anxiously on them.

"Do any of you know of anyone who went horseback riding today on my palomino pony?" Night Wolf asked loudly. "If so, please step forward."

When no one responded, Night Wolf and Brave Hawk exchanged nervous glances.

Night Wolf again looked over the crowd. "Have any of you seen Blue Star?" he asked, growing cold inside when the reply was also a negative one.

Night Wolf and Brave Hawk broke into a run and did not stop until they reached the river. Slowly they scanned the riverbank for any signs of Blue Star.

"We must gather together a search party," Night Wolf said, already running with Brave Hawk back to the village. "We must look wide and far for her."

Again Night Wolf and Brave Hawk stood together in the center of the village beside the lodge fire. Everyone crowded around them listening as Night Wolf explained about Blue Star's disappearance and the blood that was found on Night Wolf's steed.

Warriors mounted their horses. They split in two directions. They scanned the land, searched the forest and beneath the bushes, then gathered again. No one had found Blue Star or any signs of her. The longer they looked, the more their hopes waned.

There was one last place to look. Fort Harris.

They rode hard until they reached a bluff that overlooked the fort. Night Wolf and Brave Hawk stared down at it.

"Could someone from there have harmed her?" Night Wolf wondered. "Or a renegade who might be holding her captive?"

"Do you have any enemies who might do

this for vengeance?" Brave Hawk asked. "Do you have enemies at the fort?"

"I am a man of peace," Night Wolf said. "If I have enemies, they have not made themselves known to me."

Then he looked over at the trading post. "Except for one man," he said, staring at the large cabin but seeing no activity there.

His gaze went to Marissa's window. He ached for her.

"Except for one man?" Brave Hawk said, breaking through Night Wolf's thoughts "Whom do you speak of? Is it someone who would take an innocent woman captive?"

"*Gah-ween*, no, it is not that sort of antagonism that flows between me and the man. Not the sort that would cause him to take a woman captive," Night Wolf said. He sighed. "Forget him. Let us focus on who might have Blue Star and what we should do about it."

"Do you think that the abductor is a man with red skin or white?" Brave Hawk asked.

"I do not know of any white men in this area who have taken Indian women or men," Night Wolf said. "Blue Star *must* be a captive. There are no signs of her anywhere."

"Then you know what we must do," Brave Hawk said, his voice rising with anger.

"*Ay-uh*, yes, we must return home and have

a prayer council. Then we must travel to the nearest Indian camp to see if they have taken Blue Star as their captive," Night Wolf said. "If she is not there, then we will travel to the next, and then the next. If we do not find her at the camps, then we will consider that it was a white man who did this and search him out. We will rescue Blue Star and make the man who is responsible pay."

"If blood is spilled again, we must make certain it is not my sister's, but instead the blood of those who are responsible for spilling hers!" Brave Hawk said, his teeth clenched angrily.

They wheeled their horses around and headed toward home, already thinking of being forced onto the warpath, something that Night Wolf had always avoided. But if necessary, all of his and Brave Hawk's warriors' faces would be painted black. They would chant and sing the war songs of their people's pasts.

Night Wolf could not help but hold himself responsible for whatever happened to Blue Star. Had he still planned to marry her, she would be at his village, a sweet smile on her face.

As it was, he had no idea if she was even still alive.

Chapter 24

Marissa was glad to smell smoke, which she knew must be coming from the Cree's lodge fires. It meant that she was close. She had not been concerned about coming across Bradley in the forest. She didn't think that he would ever do anything to harm her, since he knew that doing so would go against his future aspirations of becoming a powerful colonel. But she was glad to have finally reached her destination. She would never forget Father Mulvaney telling her not to tempt fate.

No matter, she had something to do for someone else's benefit. Blue Star had come through a traumatic experience. The Chippewa maiden should have her family with her now. And it was up to Marissa to see that that happened.

She only hoped that Blue Star would come to see her in a different light. She could not help it that the man Blue Star had planned to marry had fallen in love with her. But she could step aside and forget Night Wolf. Perhaps if she did, he might marry Blue Star.

Although it broke her heart to picture Blue Star and Night Wolf together, Marissa knew that a sacrifice must be made.

She knew that she must let him go.

For a moment, after learning that Night Wolf had told Blue Star that he could not marry her, Marissa had envisioned herself and Night Wolf together, as man and wife, as having children together.

But that had been for only a moment in time. She knew that she had no place in Night Wolf's life. She would have to make do with what life had handed her and what it might hand her in the future.

She was young. She had been told many times how pretty she was. She would find another man and be content.

Brushing tears from her eyes, she rode onward. As she came to the edge of the Cree village, she saw a circle of warriors dancing around the huge outdoor fire. Their faces were painted with streaks of black. She could only surmise that they were painted for war. The warriors were planning to make the person responsible for Blue Star's abduction pay.

Shivers raced up and down Marissa's spine

when she thought that Night Wolf might be a party to such a thing. He had spoken more than once of being a chief who fought for peaceful solutions to problems, not those that would take him and his men into a fight.

Almost afraid now to go on, Marissa paused for a moment longer. Then she rode on into the village.

The warriors stopped their dance and chanting, and watched her approach. The women and children stood up to see.

Night Wolf stepped away from the others and came to her. Marissa stared at his painted face and his breechclout and moccasins. She was used to seeing him wear full buckskin attire. It was as though she was looking at someone else—a stranger.

Yet when he gazed at her with his jet-black eyes, she felt the same mystical feelings exchanged between them. She dismounted quickly and went to him.

She wished she could embrace him, for their one embrace was still so vivid in her mind, so wonderful. Yet she knew that all eyes were on them now and that it was best to stand her ground.

"Why are you here?" Night Wolf asked as he saw the wonder in her eyes at his appearance.

"I have come to bring you news of Blue

Star," Marissa said, hearing the gasps all around her, confirming that the interrupted ceremony was all because of the Cree maiden.

"You know of my sister?" Brave Hawk said, hurrying to Night Wolf's side. He gazed questioningly at Marissa. "Where is she? Why is she not here? Why did she not come with you?"

Marissa nervously twisted her horse's reins in her fingers. "First let me say that Blue Star has been injured, but she is alive and safe in the hands of Father Mulvaney at the mission."

"Injured?" Brave Hawk said, his hands becoming tight fists at his sides. His eyes narrowed angrily. "How is she injured? How *was* she? And by whom?"

"She fell from her horse," Marissa said, wanting to ease some of the tension in the air by omitting some facts.

"That is how she was injured?" Night Wolf asked, heaving a sigh. "What sort of injury?"

"She ran into a low-hanging limb of a tree," Marissa said, looking from Night Wolf to Brave Hawk, then back again. "It threw her from her horse. She injured her head on the limb, and her ankle was sprained when she fell to the ground."

"She is so injured that she did not come to our home but went instead to the priests'?" Brave Hawk asked.

"The mission was much closer than your village," Marissa answered. "I found her and took her to the mission myself, but only after she agreed to go there."

"I must go to her and bring her home," Brave Hawk said, already turning to his horse.

"There is more that you need to know," Marissa said. She flinched when she saw Brave Hawk stop to give her a dark frown.

"More?" he said. He walked slowly back toward her. "What more could there be?"

Marissa felt uncomfortable about being the one to tell this part of the story. All of the Cree and Chippewa were looking at her, listening and waiting to hear.

Night Wolf stepped up to her and took one of her hands. "Continue," he urged. "Tell it all to us. You are brave to have come here alone to bring this information to us. Thank you, Marissa. Thank you for saving Blue Star and for bringing us the news about her."

"The rest of what I must say is . . . is ugly," Marissa said, still not used to seeing Night Wolf with war paint on his face and dressed in a breechclout.

But she had to admit to herself, it made him look mysteriously intriguing. She wanted to be free to love him. Now she was afraid that she had truly seen to it that she and Night Wolf could never be together. He would surely marry Blue Star to make up for what had happened to her today.

"Ugly?" Brave Hawk repeated, frowning darkly.

Marissa nodded, then told how she had found Blue Star and gave the description of the man who chased her. She explained that her father was reporting this man to Colonel Payton James, who would immediately lock the man up because of his evil deeds against Blue Star.

"This man who did this to my sister—you are certain he will be punished for what he did?" Brave Hawk asked in a low growl.

"I can never be certain about anything. But, yes, I know that you have nothing else to fear from him as far as your sister is concerned." Marissa tried to reassure Brave Hawk, yet a part of her wondered if she was telling the truth.

If Bradley went unpunished, she was afraid of what Brave Hawk and Night Wolf might do. They surely would not let the man get away with what he did without paying for it.

"We thank you, Marissa, and we are very grateful that you came to us about Blue Star," Night Wolf said. "We were ready to go and fight whoever did this. We were ready to accuse the wrong party."

"But now you know the truth, and you have to concern yourself only with getting Blue Star home and seeing to her injuries," Marissa said.

"Yes, and we will be going now," Night Wolf said, nodding at Brave Hawk. "You and I will go. We can tell the warriors to cleanse their bodies of war paint."

He smiled at Marissa. "We will gladly escort you back to your home as we go for Blue Star."

"I am so glad to have helped," Marissa said. She watched as he and Brave Hawk spoke to their warriors, then went to the river to remove the war paint.

Soon she was riding with Brave Hawk and Night Wolf. It felt so good to be with Night Wolf, and to know that she had helped him, even though she also knew she could never actually have him.

But she would take what time she could with him now, for it might be the last. She knew that now Night Wolf would marry Blue Star. Surely he felt so terrible, perhaps even responsible, for what had happened to the Chippewa maiden, that he would want to protect her from such a thing happening ever again.

Marrying her would be the best way possible to protect her. It was obvious to Marissa that he cared a lot for Blue Star, and that Night

Wolf and Blue Star's brother were endearing friends. Didn't friends sometimes go to extra lengths to make friends happy?

She was disappointed when they arrived at the mission so quickly. She would have loved having a little more time with Night Wolf.

She doubted that she would feel free to go to the Cree village again, where she had hoped to discover her true birth mother.

If she did go, it would only inflict more hurt on her, as she would always come face-to-face with Night Wolf—the man she was destined to meet but never to have.

Chapter 25

Cigar smoke spiraled into the air as Joseph awaited Colonel Payton James's response to his revelations. He sat stiffly in the chair opposite Payton, who sat behind his desk. The cigar clasped between Payton's teeth made a smoke screen between the two men.

This irritated Joseph. He had never been one to enjoy the taste of cigars, especially the rank odor or the smoke, much less having it blown directly into his face. When he and Payton were young and trying new things, Joseph had gotten ill from smoking a cigar. He had vowed never to smoke them, but Payton, from that point on, had taken up the habit for a lifetime.

"I see you still have a distaste for cigars," Payton said, idly stamping the cigar out in an ashtray. "Sorry about that, partner. I forgot."

"We've been apart for some years, Payton. There's a lot we have surely forgotten about each other. But honor, trust, and loyalty weren't among those things," Joseph said, relaxing more as the smoke began to thin. "Trust, Payton, is something that was always strong between us. It's no different now. Right?"

"Sure as hell is," Payton said, leaning back in his chair, rocking slowly.

"Then trust me when I say that son of a bitch Bradley Coomer is responsible for harming a Chippewa woman. He would have probably raped her, perhaps even killed her, had he not heard a horse approaching," Joseph said dryly. "Her description of her assailant fits Bradley perfectly and you know it. Unless there is someone else at the fort that fits the description better? If so, you have your guilty party. If not, Bradley sure as hell is the one."

"Whoa, hold on there with those accusations," Payton said, leaning forward, his brilliant violet eyes narrowing. "How can you trust the woman? What if it is one of her kind who did it and she wants to cast the blame on someone of our color to prevent a war between her people and those of the man who assaulted her?"

"Now do you truly believe that?" Joseph said, his eyes flashing angrily. "Or do you just not want to accept that your protégé could be capable of such a heinous act?"

Joseph cleared his throat, then said, "I

trusted this man enough to let him marry my daughter. I'm sure you've wondered about the chip in his tooth."

"He said he got it in a skirmish, which I always assumed was a conflict with an Indian warrior," Payton mumbled. "He seemed proud of it."

"Well, he damn well shouldn't be," Joseph growled. "While wrestling an Indian woman to the ground, the woman hit him in the mouth with a rock. *That's* how his tooth was chipped. You can only imagine what happened after that. I don't need to paint you a picture, do I?"

"I know that Bradley couldn't do such a thing as rape," Payton said stiffly. "If that's what you're implying."

Payton's jaw tightened. "You spoke of trust a moment ago," he went on. "Well, damn it, Joseph, I trust Bradley implicitly. He has never given me cause not to, and I have known him for many years. He was my protégé before I came to Fort Harris. I requested that he be stationed here. He was with me at the last fort. I singled him out because of his honorable behavior and his eagerness to be the best soldier a man could be. He reminded me of myself when I was younger. The military meant more to me than anything else. As you might notice, I stayed single because of it. I felt that a wife would only get in the way of my advancement in the military. As you yourself realized, after you got married all of your aspirations to become a powerful colonel faded away. Am I right or wrong?"

"I wouldn't trade my life with my wife and daughter for all the titles in the world," Joseph growled out.

"No regrets?" Payton asked.

"None whatsoever," Joseph said, flinching somewhat when he realized that wasn't altogether true. He regretted having returned to this territory. Because of that decision, his relationship with his beloved daughter had become strained.

And more than that. Marissa now knew things he had hoped she would never discover.

But it was too late to think about that. He couldn't take back what he had told Bradley. Things would never be the same between him and Marissa because of it.

Joseph leaned forward, his eyes narrowing in anger. "You're trying to sidetrack the reason I'm here, Payton," he said tightly. "Listen again to what I said. A man fitting Bradley's description accosted a woman—and not just any woman, an Indian. Had he succeeded in raping her, there would be an Indian uprising. You'd not be able to sit smugly behind that desk any longer idly smoking cigars. You'd have to go out and fight for your survival. So, Payton, don't you think you'd best arrest that young man before he does something that stupid again?"

"How can you talk so viciously of the man you singled out for your daughter to marry?" Payton snarled.

"Thank God I found out early enough, or my daughter's life might have been in danger every day she was married to that rogue," Joseph said. "Thankfully, he proved the sort of man he is before exchanging vows with Marissa."

"I still say you are wrong about Bradley," Payton said.

He leaned forward, his eyes level with Joseph's. "Don't you see how it might be possible for that Indian woman to lie?" he asked. "She was probably accosted by one of her own kind, perhaps a Blackfoot. They are known to have been the primary enemy of the Cree through the years. She is blaming one of my soldiers to keep her people from having a confrontation with the Blackfoot."

He shrugged. "Or maybe it was a renegade, and she's afraid to point a finger at him, for fear of his coming back and finishing what he started," he said.

"What's going on here?" Bradley asked, boldly walking into the room without knocking. He plopped down on a chair beside Joseph and looked slowly from one man to the other. "I've never seen you two look so serious during a discussion."

"Well, Bradley, maybe that's because what we are discussing isn't all that pleasant," Joseph said, his eyes narrowing as he glared at the young major. "Where have you been all day? Can anyone vouch for you? Tell us the truth about what you've been up to."

Bradley's back stiffened. He looked at Joseph guardedly. "What on earth are you talking about?" he asked. "Why do I sense that you are ready to accuse me of something?"

"Because I am, and because I'm not only accusing you, I'm saying that you are damn guilty," Joseph said, rising from the chair. He glared down at Bradley. "I trusted you enough to want you as my son-in-law, while all along you weren't worthy of wearing the uniform of the United States cavalry, much less of being a husband to any decent woman."

Bradley jumped up from the chair, his eyes wide and anxious. "What are you getting at?" he asked. "Spit it out."

"My daughter found a Chippewa woman in the forest," Joseph said tersely. "She had been ambushed by a soldier. The description she gave to my daughter was you. Bradley, you might as well confess the truth. You did it. No one at this fort has your same description."

"She's lying," Bradley stammered. "She made it up. I was horseback riding, alone. I didn't even see a woman, much less accost one."

"See? What did I tell you?" Payton said, rising from his chair. He went to Bradley and placed an arm around his shoulder. "I knew that Bradley couldn't do that to a woman."

"The one way to prove the woman is wrong is to go to the mission, where she is recovering, and let her take a look at you," Joseph said dryly. "If she says she was wrong, so be it. If not, you should be locked away."

"I will not allow Bradley to be put in such a position as that. I know that he couldn't have done this," Payton said. "If what I think is true, she would say that Bradley did it just to cover up the truth of who actually did. No. I won't ask Bradley to be humiliated in such a way. I know he is innocent."

Joseph couldn't believe that Payton could be so protective and trusting of his protégé. Yet he was, and Joseph knew that nothing he said now would change Payton's mind. But Joseph knew without a doubt that Bradley was responsible.

Bradley had made it known how he felt about Indian women when he had changed his mind about marrying Marissa upon discovering that she was part Indian. Joseph knew that Bradley could taunt a red woman in such a way.

"Joseph, look elsewhere for your guilty party," Payton said, still holding his arm around Bradley's shoulder, as though to protect him.

Joseph saw the uneasiness in Bradley's eyes as he studied the young man. Joseph knew that Bradley was the guilty party, all right, but he was torn about what to do.

For now, he would wait and watch. If Bradley was guilty, he would let down his guard eventually, and then everyone would know his true worth. Then he could pay for the crime.

Joseph nodded a silent good-bye to the colonel, frowned at Bradley, and left the office.

Once outside, he turned and stared at the colonel's window. He stiffened when he found Bradley staring back at him.

At the look in Bradley's eyes, a coldness rushed into Joseph's heart. He would not linger in this area any longer. He would pack his and Marissa's bags and get ready for the arrival of the next riverboat to take them back to Kansas where they could put all of this behind them. He wanted to get her away, not only from the likes of Bradley Coomer but also from the handsome Cree chief—and from the possibility of her finding her true mother.

He was willing to lose everything, even his dream of having his trading post in a land he loved, to assure his daughter's safety and well-being. He would willingly give it all up.

He headed back toward his home, to begin packing, to make definite plans for leaving.

Chapter 26

Colonel Payton James stared at the door after Joseph left, then slowly turned his eyes to Bradley. He studied him for a moment and noted how uneasy he was. But who wouldn't be after being accused of such a heinous crime?

Payton lifted his half-smoked cigar from the ashtray and relit it. He took two deep drags, and as smoke rose in slow curls toward the ceiling, he again gazed at Bradley.

"You don't believe him, do you?" Bradley finally asked, feeling more uneasy by the minute as Payton continued a questioning gaze. "Do you actually believe that I would do anything that would threaten my career in the cavalry? I want to follow in your footsteps and become the powerful colonel that you are. I would never do anything to jeopardize it."

"I know that," Payton said, nodding. "And so should Joseph. I've told him about you enough times. He admired you enough to want you for his son-in-law. So don't fret over what he said. After he thinks about it some more, he'll realize his mistake."

"And what if he persists in believing that I did it?" Bradley said, his voice drawn. "What can I do to prove my innocence?"

"Go to the Indian woman and ask her to admit that she lied," Payton said, again setting his cigar on the edge of the ashtray.

Bradley's throat constricted at the suggestion. He was feeling trapped. What if Payton offered to go with him and was there when the Indian woman showed her loathing of him? It would be proof that he had lied, not her.

"I don't think I want to go anywhere near that woman," Bradley said. "If she can lie so easily, won't she continue with that lie? No. I don't want to put myself in the position of being accused, especially when I'm not guilty."

"Whatever happens, I don't think Joseph will accept you into his family as a son-in-law now," Payton said, sighing. "So you'd best forget Marissa."

Bradley stiffened, for it was obvious that Joseph hadn't told Colonel James about the confrontation they had had when Joseph revealed Marissa's true parentage.

Bradley didn't believe that he should bring that up now. Payton would find out soon enough.

Bradley knew that Joseph would tell him. More than likely Joseph had been ready to tell Payton about the change today just as Bradley interrupted their little tête-à-tête. His timing had been perfect, but he knew that he was only putting off the inevitable by not telling Payton now.

But time was what he needed. At this moment time might be his only friend.

"I have a meeting," Payton said, rising from his chair. He went around the desk and rested a hand gently on Bradley's shoulder. "If you need to talk some more about this, come after my meeting. It shouldn't be long."

"I'm all right with things," Bradley said, rising from the chair. He was glad when Payton pulled him into a hug. The colonel believed him—or at least he wanted to.

Payton went to the door and opened it, then stood aside as Bradley smiled and left the room.

Bradley could feel Payton's eyes on him as he walked to the door. He was relieved when he finally got outside and could be alone with his rage at Joseph McHugh.

Because of Joseph, Bradley's world was slowly unraveling. First he had sprung the truth about Marissa being part Indian. Then he pointed an accusing finger at him about what had happened to the Indian woman.

Of course Joseph was right to tell Bradley about Marissa. Who would want to take the chance of having a child whose skin proved its mother was a breed? And of course the man was right about his suspicions of Bradley's behavior with the Indian woman.

But he was purposely trying to ruin Bradley, and that made him hate Joseph with a passion. Bradley not only wanted to silence the Indian woman forever, he wanted to make certain Joseph didn't interfere in his life again. Right now he had Colonel Payton James on his side. He could not chance anything happening that might change that.

He heard someone arriving at the mission on horseback and jerked his head in that direction to see who it was.

His heart lurched when he saw that it was Marissa. She was with Night Wolf and another Indian he was unfamiliar with. He watched until they went inside the mission.

Worried that they planned to come to the fort to lodge a complaint against him, Bradley hurried toward his horse. He would soon lose everything he had always dreamed of, all because he had almost killed an Indian woman.

He had much to think about as he rode into the dark shadows of the forest.

Chapter 27

Marissa stood back as brother and sister were reunited. She was aware of Night Wolf standing close to her. She could smell his familiar scent, that of clean river water and fresh air, and a manly scent that she had noticed that first time she was near him.

It was hard to stand there and not look at him or speak to him. It was hard not to turn to him and apologize for so many things, and reveal to him just how much she loved him.

She knew that he was free to love anyone he chose, even her, yet it just did not seem that things could ever work out between them.

For now, she tried to focus on Blue Star. Her heart went out to the injured Indian maiden as Blue Star sobbed while telling Brave Hawk what had happened to her.

Again Marissa cringed at the thought of marrying such a man as Bradley Coomer. She hoped her father understood how wrong he had been and would never try to marry her off again. She was a woman. She had her own desires. Her own wishes.

She only hoped that she would find courage enough to follow her heart and put everything behind her.

But now there was something else to add to the strain between herself and Night Wolf. Blue Star's experience in the forest was perpetrated by a white man.

Surely some sort of vengeance would be taken, perhaps against the entire white community.

She tried not to think farther on that possibility, but centered her attention on Blue Star as she continued telling about the assault and how it had frightened her.

"I will seek vengeance for what was done to you," Brave Hawk said, his arms around his sister protectively. "No one does this to my sister and lives to talk about it."

Panic in her voice and eyes, Blue Star jerked free of Brave Hawk's arms. "*Gah-ween*, no!" she cried. "Please do not do anything. We have just arrived to this area. I do not want to be the cause of a war with the whites. I was wrong to be alone in a new land. It was a temptation to anyone who resents people with our skin coloring. Big brother, I will not do this again. Just please take me to our people. Forget all of this—not forgive, just forget."

"Is that what you truly want?" Brave Hawk asked, gently placing his hands on her shoulders. "Little sister, how can you not want vengeance?"

"Vengeance for one thing could build vengeance for many more things," Blue Star said, her eyes wavering. "Big brother, please take me to our people. I find such solace in their presence. They will help me forget."

"Then that is what I will do for you," Brave Hawk said. He turned to Marissa. "Thank you for saving my sister's life. We are in your debt."

"No, please don't think of it in that way," Marissa said, blushing. "I was glad to do this for Blue Star. I am relieved that she is going to be all right."

"I will have trouble walking for a while, but *ay-uh*, yes, I will be all right," Blue Star said, smiling genuinely at Marissa. "Friends? Are we friends again?"

"Yes, now and for always if that is what you wish," Marissa said, going to Blue Star. As Brave Hawk stepped aside, Marissa leaned down and hugged Blue Star. "I am so glad that I found you."

"Had you not . . ."

"No, don't think that."

Brave Hawk lifted Blue Star into his arms, and Father Mulvaney handed him a small bag.

"Your sister's clothes," the priest said. "I believe they are too soiled to wear again, but nevertheless, they are hers."

"Thank you," Brave Hawk said. He nodded toward Night Wolf. "Please give the bag to my friend. He will take it home for me. My hands are full." He gave the priest a grateful smile. "Thank you for everything. I will think of a way to repay you."

Father Mulvaney said, "It is payment enough to see that she is going to be all right."

Brave Hawk turned back to Night Wolf. "Are you ready to leave?"

"I will follow soon, but I wish to stay here a while longer," Night Wolf said. "I need to talk with Marissa."

Brave Hawk gave him a knowing nod, then left the mission.

Father Mulvaney excused himself and left. Marissa and Night Wolf were alone.

"I want to thank you myself for what you did for Blue Star," he said.

"I was happy to," Marissa replied, her heart thudding.

She was alone with Night Wolf and so close. She quietly prayed that he would embrace her again. But then she would have to say that dreaded good-bye. She knew that it was best not to seek further relations with him.

"Accompany me to my village," Night Wolf said, devouring her with his eyes, wishing to hold and kiss her. But he had to practice restraint now. He knew that this was not the time or the place. He hoped fervently that the opportunity would arise again.

"Accompany you?" Marissa gulped

"Yes," Night Wolf said. "Be a part of the happiness that you have brought my people and the Chippewa. You have saved one of their beloved maidens."

Marissa wanted to say yes. She wanted to go with him. But she knew that she shouldn't. She had to fight her feelings for him even though she now knew that he didn't love Blue Star and wasn't going to marry her.

But Blue Star's feelings about his decision were still too raw. Marissa couldn't flaunt their relationship in her face by going to the village with Night Wolf. The last thing Marissa wanted was to lose Blue Star's friendship again, after having another chance.

"I can't," she answered.

"Is there a reason you wish to tell me?" Night Wolf asked, feeling the rejection deep in his heart.

"Not right now," Marissa said, then ran out of the mission toward her home.

She knew that Night Hawk must be confused about her decision. She wasn't sure why she felt compelled to hurt him over and over again. It was just that she was torn about everything. When she made a move toward him, she wanted it to be at the right time and at the right place.

She stiffened when she heard him ride away.

She wondered what was in his mind and heart. Would he hate her now? Would he ever speak to her again? Had she just lost the opportunity to be with him, to be held by him?

Sobbing, she ran through the back door of the trading post. She stopped abruptly when she saw packed bags and trunks. Her personal trunk sat closed in the corridor.

"What does this mean?" she whispered. Then it came to her. She knew exactly what it meant!

Chapter 28

Marissa was still staring at the trunks when her father came from his study.

"And so now you know," he said, his voice tight. "I have no choice, Marissa. We've got to go back to Kansas City. A riverboat should be arriving soon. It will be the last until spring. We will be on it."

"No. I can't believe you are doing this," Marissa said, her pulse racing at the thought of never seeing Night Wolf again, never finding her true mother.

"Like I said, Marissa, I have no choice," Joseph said, coming to her. He tried to draw her into his arms but flinched when she yanked away and glared at him.

"Marissa, I hate having to abandon my project, give it to someone who could never love trading or this post as much as I do. But I have to get you back to a tame, sane country. This land is too wild for someone like you."

"Like me?" she cried. "Father, this is my *true* home, and you know it. I was born here. My mother is surely near. I want to know her, and her people, and I will."

She was surprised at what she had just said, for it had been without much thought. But she was adamant about her decision.

Although she had decided not to pursue her feelings for Night Wolf, or to go to his village again, she knew that she had only been fooling herself.

Her father's sudden plans to return to Kansas made her realize just how much she wanted to stay in the area, and how important it was to her to search for her mother.

And Night Wolf?

She would no longer deny her feelings for him. He wanted her. She wanted him. She would go to him and let him know that she was ready to make a commitment if he still wanted her.

"Father, what you have just done has worked in my favor, but not in the way you planned," Marissa said, her insides tightening when she saw the hurt and alarm in his eyes. She knew he expected her to say what he did not want to hear. "Father, I am going to the Indian village now. Do not come after me. I will return by nightfall. I promise."

She stared at the bags again, especially her personal trunk, and turned back to her father. "You might as well unpack those things. I am not going back to Kansas," she said softly. "Father, I love you, but this time I must follow my heart."

She ran to him and hugged him. "You know that you don't want to go back to Kansas either," she said. She backed away from him, her eyes pleading. "You planned your trading post for so long, I won't let you abandon it. And, Father, please, please understand my feelings about things. I have to know my true heritage."

Her jaw tightened as she took another step back from him. "And I want to see if it is too late for me with Night Wolf," she said, swallowing hard. "I have treated him so coldly I doubt he will even speak to me, much less accept my apology. I cannot help but love him."

She flinched when she saw the color drain from his face. "Yes, Father," she murmured. "Love. I fell in love with that man the first time I saw him. He loves me, too. I know it. He canceled his plans to marry Blue Star because of me. I—I—felt badly for Blue Star when I discovered that Night Wolf had told her that he couldn't marry her, but now I think she understands why he did. He loves me. It would be wrong to marry someone else."

"I can't believe I am hearing this." Joseph gulped. He gestured toward Marissa, yet did not go to her. "Daughter, please don't do this. It's not that I dislike Indians, I—just know how you will be looked at—treated by—the white community. No white woman marries a redskin without being ostracized for it."

"Just how many white people do you see in this area who could do that to me?" Marissa asked. "Yes, there are those at the fort. But how often do they cross our paths? Father, even if settlers came to this area and built a town close to the Cree village, I would still hold my head up in their presence. I could never be ashamed of the person I love."

"But there will be children," Joseph said, his eyes wavering.

"Yes, and they will be your grandchildren," Marissa said, smiling softly at him. "Father, how often have you told me that you could hardly wait to be a grandfather? Would it truly matter if their skin color was different from yours? It did not matter to you when you knew that I was part Indian. You took me in and loved me. Wouldn't you love children born of my love with Night Wolf?"

"You know that I would," Joseph said gently. "But aren't we both getting ahead of ourselves? Night Wolf might resent me so much, and perhaps the way you have treated him, that he won't consider marrying you now."

"I hope you are wrong," Marissa said, sighing. "I do love him so much. I plan to go to him now and tell him."

"I see that I have no choice but to step aside and allow you to go," Joseph said, his voice breaking. "I love you so much, Marissa. I will try to understand your feelings about all this."

He took her hands in his. "But you must let me ride with you to the village," he said. "I can't get what happened to Blue Star out of my mind."

"But, Father, the man who did that is surely behind bars as we speak," Marissa said. Her eyes widened when she saw her father's reaction. He withdrew his hands. His eyes narrowed and his jaw tightened.

"Daughter, he's not behind bars now, nor will he ever be if Payton James has anything to say about it," Joseph said. "Marissa, Payton didn't believe that Bradley did the accosting. Nothing I said convinced him. Bradley is still free to come and go as he pleases. He will never pay for what he did. That means he is free to do it again should he decide to."

"What?" Marissa paled. "Colonel James believed Bradley over you? How can that be?"

"Because Payton didn't want to think

Bradley could do such things, that's why," Joseph growled.

"James called you a liar?" Marissa asked.

"Not in so many words. He just said I was 'mistaken,'" Joseph said, sliding his hands into his back pockets.

"Then whom did he cast blame on?" Marissa asked.

"He said that more than likely someone of Blue Star's own kind, an Indian, perhaps a renegade, did it and that she lied because she didn't want to cause trouble between tribes," Joseph said. "Even though she described Bradley specifically enough that no one could doubt that she had seen the man, Payton just would not believe that Bradley could be responsible."

"Then he *is* free to do it again," Marissa said, shivering at the thought.

"Well, I doubt that he would do anything anytime soon," Joseph said. "He'd be dumb as hell if he did. If an accusing finger was pointed twice at him, he'd not be able to get away with it a second time."

"Do you think it is safe enough for me to travel to the Cree village? You don't think I have to worry about Bradley?" Marissa asked him.

"I think you are safe enough as far as

Bradley is concerned, but who is to say there aren't others out there ready to do the same sort of evil deed?" her father said. "I'm going to accompany you."

"No, Father, I don't want you to," Marissa insisted. "This is something I want to do on my own. I want to go to Night Wolf and apologize to him. I want to seek out my true mother. If you were there, you would put a strain on all that I want to accomplish."

Joseph studied her uncertainly.

"Father, you know that I am capable of taking care of myself," Marissa said. She slipped a hand into her right pocket and took out her pistol. "I have my pistol. I'll use it if I must."

His eyes widened as she put the pistol away, then reached inside her other pocket and withdrew the tiny beaded Indian necklace.

"I am taking the necklace with me," she said. "It is the only proof I have of who I am. If my mother is at the Cree village, she will soon know that she has come face-to-face with her daughter."

"And then?" Joseph asked guardedly.

"Then I hope she will claim me as hers," Marissa said, sliding the necklace back into her pocket.

Joseph suddenly drew her into his embrace. "I love you so much," he said, his voice breaking. "I—I feel as though I am losing too much of you to your other world. Please tell me that I am not."

"You aren't," Marissa said, returning his warm hug. "You are and always will be my father. I could never love anyone as I love you. You are so beloved to me, Father."

"Those words put such joy inside my heart," Joseph said, a sob lodging in his throat.

He stepped away from her and grabbed a rifle that he kept leaning against the wall in case of an emergency. He slapped the rifle into her hand.

"I know you have a pistol, but take this rifle as well," he said. "Use it, Marissa. Use it if the likes of Bradley Coomer crosses your path and threatens you."

"I will, Father," Marissa said. "And thank you for trusting me enough to let me go alone to the village."

"I trust you in everything," Joseph said.

"I'll be back before nightfall," Marissa said, smiling, then turned and left the cabin.

She felt her father's eyes on her at the door as she placed the rifle in the gun boot at the side of her horse, then mounted and rode away. Her heart thundered at the thought of seeing Night Wolf again and at the possibility of coming face-to-face with her true mother.

She felt as free as the wind that blew her hair and no less spirited than a bounding bobcat. She loved this wild freedom, her overflowing spirit. She loved it that she was going to the man she adored.

She looked carefully around her as she rode into the darker shadows of the forest, then followed the avenue of the river, which would take her to the Cree village. Her stomach felt weak, just as it always had when she was a child ready to do something wonderful, yet frightening.

But now, she was a woman hungering for a man. And not just any man. Night Wolf!

Chapter 29

Joseph stood at the door, watching Marissa until she was out of sight, then went to his study to get his holstered pistols.

Although Marissa wanted to travel alone, Joseph was just not ready to believe that Bradley had become civil after having accosted the Indian woman.

Bradley had Payton fooled now, but it wouldn't take much for Payton to believe his old friend about a soldier gone bad a second time.

Hurrying out of the house, Joseph saddled his horse as quickly as possible and was soon riding into the forest where he had seen Marissa enter. He made sure she was far enough ahead of him that she wouldn't hear him.

He would follow Marissa until she got safely to the Indian village, then lie low and wait for her to leave to follow her home.

He had kept her safe throughout her life. He would not let anything happen to her now.

Joseph didn't get far. Suddenly his path was blocked. He couldn't reach for his pistol because someone else's was aimed at him.

He glared at Bradley Coomer as the young major's lips curled into a sneer.

"Going somewhere?" Bradley taunted, inching his steed closer to Joseph's. "I had intended to follow Marissa until she got far enough away from the trading post, then teach her a thing or two. But I think I'd have just as much fun doing the same to you, you interfering son of a bitch. Did you truly think that Payton would believe you over me? I've got him just where I want him. He'd never believe I'd be capable of doing anything underhanded."

"And how on earth do you think you're going to get away with harming me or my daughter?" Joseph said, wanting to reach for his firearm.

But any gunfire might alarm Marissa enough that she would backtrack and ride right into the face of danger.

He would have to play this one minute at a time and hope that he could get the better of Bradley before the man managed to kill him.

"I've got a plan," Bradley said, laughing loosely. "I had not figured on you being a part of it, but since you're butting in again by following your daughter, I'll deal with you first, her later."

"You stay away from my daughter or you'll have hell to pay," Joseph growled, his eyes narrowed angrily at the young major. "Payton was wrong to believe the likes of you. He should've arrested you. A man like you should be stripped of all honors."

"And you're going to see that it's done, huh?" Bradley said, chuckling again.

"I lost the argument before with Payton, but this time I plan to make my old friend see the true evil of his protégé. You must be dealt with," Joseph hissed.

"You aren't going to be telling anyone anything about me, now or ever," Bradley spat out. He nodded toward the depths of the forest. "Go on ahead of me. I'll tell you when you get where I planned to take Marissa."

"And where might that be?" Joseph asked, realizing the true danger that he was in.

"Where am I taking you?" Bradley said. "To hell."

Hearing the evil in Bradley's voice, Joseph realized that he was in the presence of a madman. He tried for his pistol, but Bradley cocked his firearm and steadied his aim at Joseph's gut.

"I wouldn't do that," Bradley said tightly. "But I do want you to get the gun. Throw your pistol over there in the weeds. Remember that I'm ready to fire should you get the notion to try and shoot at me."

His heart pounding, Joseph reached for his pistol with a shaking hand. He wanted to chance firing it, yet he remembered Marissa. She was not that far in front of him, and she would most certainly hear the report of the gun and come back to investigate.

Muttering obscenities beneath his breath, Joseph pitched his pistol into the underbrush, then slapped the reins against his horse and rode on past Bradley, who followed close behind.

"I'll be taking care of Marissa soon," Bradley said. "You and she have made a fool of me, and no one does that. I won't allow either of you to get in the way of my career as a military officer."

"And how on earth do you think you can get away with murdering me and my daughter and still seem innocent when our bodies are found?" Joseph said, looking angrily over his shoulder at Bradley. "You can't get away with this. Surely you know it."

"I'll make it look like two Indian kills,"

Bradley said, shrugging idly. "No one will know the difference."

"You're mad. *Insane*," Joseph said, wincing when Bradley raised his gun again and aimed it at Joseph's head.

He turned around and rode onward into the shadows, hoping that Marissa had made it to the Indian village. There she would find safety with Night Wolf. Surely Night Wolf wouldn't let her leave alone when she decided to return home.

This lunatic redheaded major would be waiting to ambush her.

Chapter 30

As Marissa rode slowly into the Indian village, she had a mixture of feelings. She was excited to be among her own kind of people, yet apprehensive, for what if they did not accept her once she revealed her true identity to them?

Her main concern, though, was Night Wolf. Had she insulted him one time too many? Would he invite her into his lodge to sit and talk with him, and allow her to explain her behavior? If he gave her the chance to stay long enough to show him the tiny necklace, what would his reaction be to it? Would he possibly recognize it?

Her questions spilled over one another in her mind. She forced herself to stop thinking so intensely when she realized the activity around her. On the outskirts of the village, she had seen many women harvesting the corn in the field that lay in the fertile river bottom. Some of them brought the corn into the village in large wicker baskets. Large pieces of buckskin were spread upon the grass near several tepees. Upon those lay much of the harvested sweet corn, drying beneath the late-afternoon sun.

Elsewhere women were slicing great orange pumpkins into thin rings, doubling and linking them together into long chains, then hanging them on poles that stretched between two forked posts. She assumed that they hung there for drying as well.

She saw other fruits spread out on buckskin to dry in the wind and sun. She saw cherries, berries, and plums.

Then she saw something besides the harvest. Her heart leapt into her throat, and her eyes widened when she saw Night Wolf step out of his tepee still wearing the breechclout. He quickly discovered her approaching.

She gazed into his eyes as he came toward her. His long black hair fluttered in the soft breeze, and his jet-black eyes met and held hers.

Her heart thundered as he stepped up to her horse and took the reins from her.

No words were exchanged between them as she slid from her saddle and stood so close to him that she could smell his familiar scent. It made her melt from her need of him.

He handed her horse's reins to a young

brave, who took her steed away. He gestured toward his tepee, then held the flap aside for her to enter.

Every footstep seemed clumsy as she stepped into his home.

She noticed its size, its cleanliness, and the way it smelled of him. She was in awe of everything she saw within the tepee, things that she had only read about in books.

She felt drawn into it and realized that throughout her life, something within her had tried to cry out. It was the Indian in her.

She watched Night Wolf go to the firepit and settle on his haunches beside it, his eyes slowly moving to her.

"What has brought you here?" he asked, not asking her to sit even though he had so readily shown her into his lodge.

Marissa's knees were trembling. She only hoped that her voice wouldn't when she spoke. She didn't want him to think she was afraid of him. She loved him. She wanted him. She ached for him.

"You," she blurted out.

"And why is that?" he asked.

"I came to say so much," Marissa said, beginning to feel uneasy about being there.

There was so much about his demeanor that made her think that he wished she had not come. Or else, why would he not have invited her to sit down? Standing with his eyes on her, she felt anything but welcome.

"Say it," he said, his eyes still held steady with hers.

"I'm sorry for how I've treated you," Marissa said, her voice breaking. "It was not at all how I felt, or how I wanted to behave while with you. Night Wolf, it was all because of how I was told I should behave. It was not at all like what I felt."

"And who told you to behave in this way?" he asked, already knowing the answer. But he had to hear her say it.

"Both my father and Father Mulvaney," she said, her eyes wavering.

His eyebrows rose in surprise. He had expected to hear her say her father, but Father Mulvaney?

Night Wolf was friends with Father Mulvaney. Why would he warn this lovely woman away from him?

"I understand your father's reason, but what of Father Mulvaney's?" he asked, slowly rising to his feet.

"He knew of your betrothal to Blue Star," Marissa murmured. "He told me that it was sinful of me to love a man who was promised to someone else. He told me to repent."

That was all he needed to know. He saw how she would have denied him if she thought that he loved another woman.

He went to Marissa. "Although it was sudden, I have never loved anyone but you," he said. The fire shone brightly into Marissa's face, intensifying the violet color of her eyes, the evidence of her need in their depths.

Marissa almost swooned when he framed her face between his hands. Her heartbeats were swallowing her whole as he lowered his lips to hers.

"It is right that we should love one another," he said huskily. "I have not been able to stop myself from loving you."

He brought his lips down hard upon hers in a kiss that swept all doubts from Marissa's mind.

She knew that he could forgive her wrongful behavior toward him. She no longer doubted that his love for her was true.

She twined her arms around his neck and returned the kiss with abandon. She gasped with pleasure when he brought one of his hands down between them and cupped a breast within it. She leaned into his hand, her head spinning from the wonders of how it felt for him to caress her. She was on fire, her body melting against his.

"You came, you love, let us make love," he whispered against her lips.

Those words made Marissa's insides tighten, but only for a moment. She knew that she yearned for everything he could give her. Until this moment, she had been a young girl. Now she was a woman with a woman's desires, and she knew that if they both loved one another, anything they did together was surely right.

Marissa stepped away from him, bent to remove her boots, then tossed them aside. She smiled into his eyes. She trembled as he unbuttoned her skirt, then drew it down over her hips, then lower, until it lay around her ankles on the mats beneath her bare feet.

She felt a strange ache at the juncture of her thighs. His kiss had awakened something there, something that felt deliciously wicked, yet right.

His eyes held hers in hungry intent as he slowly unbuttoned her blouse.

She closed her eyes in ecstasy and sucked in a wild breath as he opened the blouse and leaned down and flicked his tongue over a nipple. Never in her life had she felt anything as blissful.

Her senses were ignited, were reeling.

She emitted a soft cry of passion as his hand

slid down her belly, then brushed over her secret place. She moaned when he stroked her there, awakening feelings that she had never known could exist.

Then he stopped.

She opened her eyes and saw his hands at the waist of his breechclout.

She held her breath as he lowered the breechclout, then dropped it to the floor. She had never seen a naked man before. But she saw one now and knew that he was ready to love her.

She was in awe of his length and firmness.

His eyes swept over her with a silent, urgent message. His hand still caressed her, arousing feelings within her that were deliciously sweet.

Soft moans repeatedly surfaced from inside her as his fingers worked their magic on her body, and his tongue swirled around her nipples.

He enfolded her within his arms and led her down to a pallet of ermine and marten pelts. She sank deep within their softness and gazed up at Night Wolf as he knelt over her.

He brushed her hair back from her face, then kissed her with a fierce, possessive heat as he spread himself fully over her.

She clung to him and returned the kiss, aware of his manhood finding her hot, moist place. He did not enter her with one deep thrust, but instead went slowly within her, as though testing her. She scarcely breathed.

He drew his lips from hers, his eyes exploring hers, a question in their depths.

"I have never been with a man before," she murmured as though she knew what his question was. "You . . . are . . . the first."

"I will be gentle," he said huskily. "The pain will be brief, and then you will join me on a journey to the stars."

"Please hold me. Kiss me," Marissa said. "I want you. I need you."

He covered her lips tenderly with his, his arms around her holding her gently. He held her endearingly close as he made a final thrust within her that broke through the wall that proved she was a virgin—a woman who had waited for the man she loved to introduce her to lovemaking.

Marissa flinched and moaned against his lips, and her body tightened from the pain. Then she melted away as he began his thrusts, slowly and gently at first, and then plunged more eagerly into her, withdrew and plunged again. His hands enfolded her breasts, her nipples burning into his skin.

He moved his lips to a breast, his tongue rolling the nipple, his teeth nipping.

Marissa closed her eyes and felt herself floating as the passion swelled within her, spreading, building. The rhythmic pressure of his thrusts took her to a place of infinite sweetness.

Again he kissed her. She twined her arms around his neck and returned it.

He lifted her legs so that they were wrapped around him, bringing him more deeply within her as his thrusts sent ecstatic waves crashing through her.

He felt euphoria fill his entire being. He had never felt this before. He was overcome with a feverish heat, as though white flames were roaring in his ears. He heard only her voice calling his name as she drew her lips from his. She lay her cheek against his. Her soft words of encouragement drove him onward.

Suddenly his body tightened.

He paused to get his breath, and then with one last, deep plunge he felt himself going over the edge.

Their bodies trembled as they clung to that cloud and rode it into the sky, where stars seemed to be exploding.

When it was over, they lay breathlessly in each other's arms, the mystical glow still around them.

"Was it everything you wanted it to be?" he whispered in her ear.

"It was more than that," Marissa whispered.

He rolled away from her to stretch out on his back.

She moved closer to him and slowly ran a hand up and down his body, still wet with sweat. She gazed at that part of him that had taken her to paradise and back.

It was not as large now, but when she touched it, it seemed to spring back to life. She marveled at that, then smiled at him.

"Your body is wonderful," she said, giggling softly.

"Your body is *mee-kah-wah-diz-ee*, beautiful," he said.

"I love you so much," Marissa said, cuddling closer to him. "I am so glad that I came to talk with you today. Had I not . . ."

"But you are here," he said, reaching over and holding her. "Do not think about it. That is the past. This is now. We are here for each other forever."

"I fought so hard against my feelings for you," Marissa said, her voice breaking. "I was wrong to listen to anyone but my own heart."

"I understand why you fought your feelings," Night Wolf replied. "But that is now behind us. There is no reason ever to fight feelings again. I want you for my *ee-quay*, which in my language means 'wife.' I cannot live life without you."

"But Blue Star—" she began, but stopped when he placed a finger over her lips, silencing her.

"Blue Star understands that I can never marry her, and why," he said. "I had hoped that it would work because I needed a wife and a stronger alliance between my people and Brave Hawk's. But I realized that the alliance was already strong between me and my Chippewa friend. He would never want me to marry someone I did not love. Friends understand such things."

"Then the alliance will not grow weaker because you're not marrying Blue Star?" Marissa asked. She rose onto an elbow and gazed into his eyes. "Things will be all right?"

"*Ay-uh*, especially since you came to me and proved your love for me," Night Wolf said, looking directly into her eyes. "And what of your father? Will he not try everything to keep us apart? Will he allow you to be my *ee-quay*?"

Marissa looked deep into his eyes. "You want me? You want me for your wife?" she murmured.

"I would have never made love with you had I not planned to make you my wife. Nor would you have allowed me to had you not known that I would marry you," Night Wolf said. He touched her face gently. "Is that not so? When we made love, did you not know that it was because you saw us already as man and wife? You knew that we would soon be speaking vows between us."

"Yes, I knew we would," Marissa said. "And, no, I would never have made love with a man had I not known his love was sincere."

"We will marry soon, then?" he said, his eyes searching hers.

"I hope so," Marissa said.

"What about your father?" Night Wolf asked. "What sort of trouble will he cause? You know that he does not want you to be the wife of a man with skin color that is not the same as yours."

Her eyes danced. "But mine *is* the same, only one cannot see it," she said. "I *am* part Indian. My mother was Indian. And since my skin is whiter than an Indian's, my father must have been white."

Night Wolf was taken aback by what she said. He sat up quickly. He watched as she sat up as well, her eyes still smiling into his.

"You have an Indian mother?" he asked.

"Let me show you," Marissa said.

Feeling somewhat awkward about being undressed in his presence, she hurried into her clothes as he pulled his breechclout on again. Then they sat down together.

She slid a hand inside her pocket and withdrew the tiny necklace. She laid it in her palm and held it out for Night Wolf to see.

"This is the only proof of my heritage," she said, her voice breaking. "When Father found me in the forest, I had this around my neck. When he saw my thick black hair, the necklace, and the Indian blanket that I was wrapped in, he assumed I was born to an Indian woman."

"Your father found you?" Night Wolf gasped, stunned by what she was saying.

"He found me, took me home, and he and the woman I always knew as my mother left for Kansas. When they arrived there, they adopted me," Marissa said, watching his eyes for his reaction. "I didn't know until recently who I truly am. I discovered it by accident. I shall tell you how one day. But it was then that my father brought the necklace out of hiding and gave it to me. It was then that he explained how he instead of my true birth mother came to have me."

"Let me see the necklace," Night Wolf said. Marissa placed it in his outspread hand. "There is something about it that is familiar to me."

He had no time to tell her what it was. A soft

voice outside the tepee brought his eyes quickly to the closed entrance flap.

The voice spoke again, and he recognized it to be Shame on Face's.

He handed the necklace quickly to Marissa, gave her a lengthy stare, then went to the entrance flap and shoved it aside.

"I have brought word to you that Blue Star is much better," Shame on Face said, then raised a shaggy gray eyebrow as Marissa came to stand at Night Wolf's side.

Her eyes moved slowly to the necklace in Marissa's hand. Her trembling hand went to her own necklace around her neck.

Marissa gasped, as Shame on Face fell to the ground in a dead faint.

Marissa was struck speechless. The old woman's necklace was identical to hers.

She stared at Shame on Face, then with a pounding heart turned to Night Wolf.

Chapter 31

"Her name is Shame on Face," Night Wolf said as he knelt beside her.

"Shame on Face?" Marissa repeated, watching Night Wolf gently lift Shame on Face into his arms. She followed him as he carried the elderly woman into his tepee. He laid her on a pallet of pelts opposite from where Marissa and Night Wolf had just made love.

"The name . . ." Marissa said, grasping her necklace in her hand. She stared down at the woman who she believed could be her mother.

She tried to find some of her own features in the woman's face and could not. Surely, though, Shame on Face's hair had at one time been as black as Marissa's, the one thing that Marissa knew she had taken from the Indian side of her heritage.

That had to mean, then, that she had mostly her father's features.

In a state of shock over her discovery,

Marissa scarcely noticed Night Wolf pouring water into a wooden basin. He began bathing Shame on Face's face in an effort to revive her.

He gazed at the necklace in Marissa's hand, then looked at the identical necklace around Shame on Face's neck.

"I was right," he said. "The necklaces are the same in the way they were made. Marissa, Shame on Face also noticed. That is why she fainted."

"Shame on Face?" Marissa again questioned, looking at Night Wolf as he gazed over his shoulder at her. "That's a horrible name. How could anyone name their child Shame on Face when it was born?"

"She was not given the name at birth," Night Wolf said. "It was a name she gave herself after she abandoned her newborn child. She felt such shame over having done it. She has lived the life of a recluse except for her times with me and my mother. Until recently, we were the only two people she associated with for eighteen winters."

"Eighteen winters?" Marissa gasped. "She—abandoned a child—eighteen winters ago? Why?"

"It is quite a long story," Night Wolf said, stunned by what he might have just discovered. He gazed at the tiny necklace again. "I saw your father give this to you that night I brought you moccasins."

"You did?" Marissa interrupted him. "How? Why?"

"I came that night in hopes of speaking with you," Night Wolf said. "When I saw that you weren't in your room, I left the moccasins as a silent message that I had been there. I looked into another window and saw you with your father. You were discussing something as he handed you the necklace."

"Yes, we were. The necklace was around my neck on the day that he found me in the forest, where I was left—by my birth mother," she said, her voice breaking. "Father knew that if anyone saw it, it would help identify who my mother was. Instead of discarding it, he kept it. I think deep down inside he knew that I would eventually want to know the truth."

Suddenly Shame on Face reached out and clasped one of Night Wolf's hands. She gave him a questioning look then gazed past him at Marissa.

"Come closer," Shame on Face whispered to Marissa, tears flowing from her eyes.

Marissa felt frozen to the spot. She gulped hard but only stared at the woman, then at her necklace.

"Please?" Shame on Face pleaded.

Night Wolf shoved the basin of water aside and reached out to Marissa.

She looked into his eyes and knew what he was asking of her. She took his hand, then moved down beside Shame on Face as Night Wolf stepped aside and made room for her.

As his hand dropped away from hers, Shame on Face reached out to Marissa's face. Her hands trembled as she touched her daughter for the first time in eighteen winters.

"Daugher," she said, her voice quivering. "My daughter. How did you know to come to me? I have prayed to *Wenebojo* that you would come. I have longed for this moment."

The gentle touch, the love in Shame on Face's voice, drew Marissa into an instant caring for her. All bad thoughts were erased from her mind by that single touch.

"I was only recently shown the necklace," Marissa said softly. "I was told about where I was found, and that the man and woman who raised me as their own were not my true parents. At that moment I hungered to find my birth mother. When my father said that I had been found on this land in big sky country and that my mother must be Indian, I knew that I could not stop until I found you."

She swallowed hard and smiled lovingly down at Shame on Face. "I would have never guessed in a million years that I would find my mother this easily," she murmured. "But I have, haven't I? You *are* my true mother?"

"*Ay-uh*, I am your true mother," Shame on Face said. She took one of Marissa's hands, brought it to her cheek, and leaned into its palm. "My daughter. You are my daughter."

Then Shame on Face lowered Marissa's hand and clung to it just above her heart, which was pounding with happiness. "I know what your first question must be," she murmured. "You want to know if you were conceived by two people who were in love, or if by force. Daughter, you were born of love. It was an everlasting love. But your father had priorities that kept us from joining our hearts forever as man and wife."

She looked desperately into Marissa's eyes. "I have paid over and over again through the years for the crime of leaving my baby, but please listen to me," she begged, then looked at Night Wolf who sat beside Marissa. "I want you, Night Wolf, to know as well. I hope you will understand why I lived a lie all of my life. Why I forced that lie upon my own daughter."

"We are listening with open hearts," Night Wolf said, nodding. "Please continue."

Marissa was anxiously waiting as her love for this woman she knew was her mother grew.

In her heart she had already forgiven her. Her mother lived the life of a recluse, and named herself for the shame she felt for abandoning her child. She had paid for her crime. Marissa would not add to that shame by casting blame. This woman had given up everything the day she gave birth to Marissa.

"I had a love affair with a dashing white soldier," Shame on Face began, tears again streaming from her eyes as she looked beyond Night Wolf and Marissa into the past. "My husband abandoned me. He knew that the child could not be his. I was in love with the soldier, but he was not willing to sacrifice his career to marry me. Nonetheless, I knew without a doubt that he loved me."

She looked at Marissa and grasped her hand tightly. "He knew not of the child," she said, her voice breaking. "I already knew that he would never marry me, so why bring shame to us both by telling him? He was a man whose career would be endangered if anyone knew about you. I was married. In grief, I had no choice but to give up the child."

She turned her eyes away. "I lied to my people about how I conceived the child," she said solemnly. "When I began showing in my pregnancy, my people as well as my husband thought the affair had been with another Indian, not a white man. But I knew that when my child was born, the disgrace would be there for all to see. They would demand answers that I would not give them. If they had known that my lover was white, they would have killed him. I went away and had the child alone. When I saw that you were white-skinned, I had no choice but to abandon you. But I chose to leave you close to the fort. I waited long enough to see a soldier come my way. I made certain you were where he would find you. I hid and watched until he rode away with you in his arms. My heart broke, but I believed that you would be taken care of. Your skin was white. No white people would turn their back on a child whose skin was of their own kind. The necklace? I did not know that they would realize the child was part Indian because of the necklace."

She lowered her eyes. "Deep down inside, I wished that Payton would see the necklace and know the child was his, for he had often commented on mine," she said. "He would have known the necklace matched my own. I thought that perhaps if he saw the child and the necklace, he would know the baby was his and might come to me and make things right between us. But he never came. I knew then that he never would."

She looked at Marissa again. "Daughter, he was a man of kind heart, but he just could not give up everything to marry a woman with red skin," she said softly. She lowered her eyes. She cleared her throat, then looked at Marissa again. "I often thought later that I should have told Payton about the baby. I was wrong not to. But he had already broken off with me. He had already chosen his career. I could not burden him with a child he would not want."

Marissa was stunned by the story, and by the name of her mother's lover.

Payton!

She went pale when she remembered that Colonel Payton James had been a major at Fort Harris with her father, Joseph. Her father and mother had left as soon as they found Marissa. They had kept her hidden until they left the fort for Kansas.

Payton James?

Was he her true father?

She knew that he had been "married to the military" and had worked his way up to the rank of colonel.

Could it be the same man?

The eyes. Lord, Payton James's eyes were violet. So were Marissa's!

"What was my father's full name?" she asked guardedly, her eyes wavering as she saw the wonder in her mother's eyes as she gazed back at her.

"Major Payton James," Shame on Face said, her voice guarded. "He is a man who forgot me many years ago. But I have never forgotten him. Why do you ask?"

Marissa was stunned. Now she knew who both of her parents were. Her father's best friend was Marissa's true father.

Though Joseph and Payton scarcely held secrets from one another, her father had not told Payton about the child. He had thought it best not to share that secret with anyone except his beautiful, loving wife.

Numb from the knowledge, Marissa jumped to her feet and ran out of the tepee, sobbing.

Night Wolf came after her. He stopped her and turned her slowly to face him.

"The name of your true father is that of the colonel at Fort Harris," he said. "This is what has you upset?"

"Not so much upset as stunned," Marissa gulped. "Payton James is my father, yet he doesn't even know it. My father who raised me doesn't know it. What should I do?"

"Follow your heart," Night Wolf said softly. "If it tells you to go and reveal yourself as the daughter of the colonel, so be it. If it tells you to keep that hidden inside your heart, so be it."

"I must tell him," Marissa said, tears running down her face. "Don't you see? It has been unfair that neither of us knew, yet in so many ways he was always near. When there was distance between him and my father, they communicated by letters. Had they known about me, things would've been different."

"How?" Night Wolf said.

Marissa lowered her eyes. "I don't know."

She looked quickly up at him again. "I must go to him," she said. "He is my father. My father!"

"But what of your other father?" Night Wolf asked.

Marissa's eyes wavered.

Chapter 32

Marissa gazed into Night Wolf's eyes. "I am so torn," she said, her voice breaking.

"I understand how you are feeling, and I wish that I could advise you, but all I can say is follow your heart," he told her. "My woman, you do not have to rush into anything. Think it out. Be certain of your choices."

"My father never knew about me," Marissa sobbed. "He didn't turn his back on me. But he left my true mother. How could he have done that? How could he have been so callous to love her yet turn his back on her? Why didn't my mother tell him the truth about me?"

"Your mother did what she felt was right," Night Wolf said. "She did what she had to do. So did your father. By leaving the area, he stepped away from further temptation—a temptation that might have eventually ended in bloodshed. It is possible that if my people had discovered the truth, that a white soldier caused the separation of an Indian husband and wife, an uprising could have occurred. So, no, do not disrespect either your true mother or your true father. But it is up to you now, whether you go to Colonel James and tell him the truth and whether you tell your mother that the man is living in the area again."

"My mother has lived a lonely life," Marissa said, gazing toward Night Wolf's tepee where Shame on Face awaited Marissa's return. "She won't be lonely any longer. She has me now—and I am going to go to Fort Harris and tell my true father everything. They could be good for one another."

"The reason your father turned his back on your mother is the same," Night Wolf reminded her. "He is still in the military. He might still choose that over her."

Marissa's chin lifted, and her jaw tightened. "Nevertheless, I must tell them what I know," she said. "And my father has the right to know that he had a daughter, and that I am that daughter."

"But what about the man who raised you? What will his feelings be when he finds out that you have told Colonel James everything?" Night Wolf said, realizing that he was interfering in Marissa's decision when only moments ago he had said the decision must be hers to make.

"I must go to my true father and let him know about me," she murmured. "He is alone. All he has is the military. He has had that for so long, surely he hungers for something more in his life now. A daughter would fill those lonely spaces in his heart."

She smiled softly. "And since he never married, doesn't that mean that he may still love my mother? Surely since he has returned to this area he has thought of her."

"I can tell that you have made up your mind about this," Night Wolf said. He gently drew her into his arms. "My beautiful Marissa. All I want is what is best for you. If bringing your true mother and father together again is what your heart desires, then do what you must to make it possible. I promise you that none of my people will interfere. When they discover the truth about why Shame on Face abandoned her child those eighteen winters ago, they will see her as noble, for she gave up her child to keep trouble from coming into their lives. Fort Harris was the first interference in the lives of the Cree. The Cree resented it but never acted on that resentment. They will not act wrongly knowing about Shame on Face's relationship with a white pony soldier. It is far in the past."

"But if my mother and father come together as I hope they will, it will no longer be in the past, it will be the present," Marissa said. She eased herself from his arms. "Nevertheless, I must try to bring my parents together. It is a miracle that I know who they are and that they are both alive for me to love."

"You are a good woman with a big heart," Night Wolf said. "I hope that everything turns out as you wish it to. But do not be too disappointed if your father does not wish to allow the white community to know that he had an Indian lover and fathered a child."

"I am so happy to know that I was conceived out of love," Marissa sighed. "I could tell by how Shame on Face talked of their relationship. It was one of true love and devotion until my father felt that he had to make choices."

"Then you are leaving soon?" Night Wolf asked.

"Very soon. But, Night Wolf, will you please do a favor for me?" Marissa asked, her eyes searching his.

"Anything you ask of me, I will do," Night Wolf said.

"Please see that the name Shame on Face no longer applies to my mother," she murmured. "Please see that she is called by her true name."

"I shall do that for you," Night Wolf agreed.

"What is her true name?" Marissa asked.

"Soft Voice," Night Wolf said. Just then Soft Voice came out of the tepee and stood gazing at him and Marissa. She was no longer crying. She was smiling and looked the happiest he had ever seen her. There was a calm about her now, a silent grace, a glowing radiance.

"Ah, but doesn't that name fit her well?" Marissa said, as she watched Soft Voice. "Her voice is so soft, so comforting."

She walked quickly to Soft Voice and drew her into her arms. "Mother, I promise you that you will never be alone again," Marissa said, without telling her about what she had planned.

"And please allow yourself to be called Soft Voice," Marissa continued. "Not Shame on Face. I see nothing shameful about you."

"I gladly put that name to rest," Soft Voice murmured, returning Marissa's hug. "And, Marissa, please know that you were always with me. I carried you around like a precious song inside my heart."

"But now you do not have to search inside your heart to have moments with me," Marissa said. "Mother, I am here for you. I cherish the knowledge that you are my mother."

"And how do you feel about knowing who

your father is?" Soft Voice asked, stepping away from Marissa and gazing into her eyes.

"I have a mixture of feelings," Marissa answered. "My emotions are running rampant inside me. I must go and talk to him. Now that I am looking you in the eye, I feel that it is only right that you know what my plan is."

Soft Voice took a shaky step back from Marissa. "How can you go to him?" she asked, her eyes wavering. "How would you even know where he is?"

Marissa looked nervously at Night Wolf, who came and stood at her side. He gave her a nod.

"Mother, my father is stationed at Fort Harris again," Marissa said, stepping closer to her mother, taking the woman's hands in her own. "He achieved his goal in life. He is a powerful, admired colonel."

"My Payton is a colonel?" Soft Voice said, amazed at everything that had just come into her life. Her daughter, and now perhaps the man she had always loved. "He is at Fort Harris?"

"Yes," Marissa said, affectionately squeezing her mother's hands. "I am surprised to learn that Colonel James is my father, as will he be stunned to realize that I am his daughter."

Marissa swallowed hard, then said, "He

never knew that I was not the birth daughter of those who raised me. They never told him the truth."

Tears sprang to Soft Voice's eyes. "Are you going to tell him that I am here? So close that if he tried, he might hear me calling his name in my heart?"

"Do you want me to tell him that you are still in the area, and that you never took another husband?" Marissa asked.

Soft Voice was in a state of near shock. Her daughter had found her, and the man she would always love was near again.

She could not help but hunger to see him, even though she knew that he would choose his military career over her even now.

"Did he ever marry?" Soft Voice whispered.

"No, he never did," Marissa said. "When he told you that he could not help but choose the military over you, he was telling you the truth. He has never known anything but the military."

Soft Voice lowered her eyes, then looked again into Marissa's. "If you believe that he still cares for me and would like to meet with me, then I, too, am receptive to such a meeting. It would do this old heart good to look into his violet eyes again."

Her mother then reached out to stroke

Marissa's cheek. "Violet eyes," she said, smiling. "You have your father's eyes."

"Yes, I know, but I have much of you in me as well," Marissa murmured. Her smile faded. "Are you certain that you want to see Payton? He abandoned you in favor of the military. He might still feel the same way. Are you prepared if he chooses the military over you now, over seeing you one last time?"

"I want to see Payton, no matter the outcome," Soft Voice said. "I am an old lady whose years are now numbered, so I am ready for anything, even a fresh heartbreak."

"You are not all that old," Marissa said. "You are surely only in your forties."

"Yes, I am forty-one winters of age. Payton should be fifty," Soft Voice said, her voice breaking. "When we were lovers, I felt so protected by Payton. He was not only strong and muscled but mature, year-wise. *Ay-uh*, I want to see him, if he agrees to see me."

"Then I shall go to him," Marissa said, giving her mother a gentle hug.

"I shall count my heartbeats until your return," Soft Voice said, stepping away from Marissa. She slowly kneaded her brow. "I am weary. I must go to my lodge and rest. But do not hesitate to wake me if Payton comes."

"Will you feel comfortable if he comes into

the Indian village now, openly acknowledging your relationship with one another?" Marissa asked.

"It is time for this woman to get past her shame. I do not feel uncomfortable over my people knowing about Payton, both past and present relationships with him," Soft Voice said. "And I will happily announce to everyone that you are my daughter."

She sighed. "Colonel Payton James," she whispered. "He reached his goal. I am so proud for him."

"He has a remarkable personality, yet—" Marissa began, but she stopped before saying anything negative about Payton James. He had denied that Bradley was capable of the crime committed against Blue Star.

"Blue Star." Marissa looked at Night Wolf. "Do you believe she will accept that we love one another? Our marriage?"

"When she realizes that fate changed many lives today, she will understand, once and for all, why I cannot marry her," Night Wolf said. "You will be my wife, will you not? Do you have room in your heart for a husband after discovering your true mother and father?"

Marissa flung herself into his arms and melted against him. "I want to be your wife. I never could have dreamed anything as wonderful as being the wife of Chief Night Wolf of the Wolf band of Cree!"

"Your words make me happy, but there is something you must do first," Night Wolf said, stepping away from her. He gazed intently into her eyes. "Go. Tell the colonel the truth. Tell him about a woman whose husband abandoned her when he discovered her pregnancy by another man. Tell him that Soft Voice never remarried. She lived for the memory of those moments spent with Payton James. She ached inside over never knowing the fate of her one and only child."

"I must go now," Marissa said, already walking toward the corralled horses behind Night Wolf's lodge. He walked with her. "I shall be back before sundown. I hope that I will have someone with me, someone who has missed his beautiful young lover as his lover has missed him."

"I am going to accompany you to the fort," Night Wolf said as they stepped into the corral.

"That isn't necessary," she demurred. "Please stay here for Soft Voice should she need you. I shall hurry and return before you can wink an eye."

"Wink an eye?" Night Wolf said, raising an eyebrow.

Marissa giggled. "It is a saying used when

you want someone to know that you will return in haste."

"Still, I want to accompany you," Night Wolf said firmly, already taking his reins and handing Marissa's to her. He noticed the rifle in the gunboot and questioned her with his eyes.

"I see you've discovered my father's rifle," she said, swinging herself into her saddle. She patted the leather sheath that held the rifle. "As you can see, I have ways of protecting myself." She then patted the lump in her right pocket. "I also have a hand pistol in my pocket. So fret not, my sweet Night Wolf. I won't allow anyone to get the best of me."

Night Wolf thought about her courage and strong will, and of her discoveries today. He understood why she would need to be alone. She still had much to sort out in her mind.

"As you wish. I will not accompany you," Night Wolf said, glancing heavenward and seeing that the sun was almost hidden behind the distant peaks of mountains. He gave her a stern look. "If you feel threatened by anyone, do not hesitate to shoot."

"I am a practiced shot," Marissa said. "My father—I mean, Joseph—taught me the art of handling and firing firearms. Please do not worry about my well-being."

He reached up to her cheek, caressed her soft

skin, then stepped back and watched her lope out of the corral. She gave him a look over her shoulder, then slapped her reins and galloped away from him.

Marissa loved the feel of the evening breeze against her face. It was invigoratingly delicious. She smiled as she thought about the revelations of today. She had found her true parents.

Yet wasn't Joseph her father? He had saved her life all those years ago when he rescued her from the forest floor and took her to his wife.

Yes, he, not Payton, had raised her. Yet she could not help but believe that Payton should have the opportunity to know her.

In her eyes, though, Joseph would always be her father.

Chapter 33

In deep thought about how her life had changed since she arrived in big sky country, Marissa was barely aware of movement in the shadows of the aspen trees on her right.

She felt as though a new life had been handed to her, which included not only her biological mother but also a man who loved her as much as she loved him.

"And my true father," she whispered, seeing Payton James in her mind's eye. She had admired him for a long time, but only because of how her father—Joseph—talked about him. Joseph had shared some of Payton James's letters with her, reading to her of Colonel James's experiences in the military. He had painted a man of valor and goodness, someone she had been eager to meet.

She had not been disappointed when she had been introduced to him. He was a well-built, handsome man, whose auburn hair had just begun to be speckled with gray. She had noticed that his eyes were the same color as hers. She hadn't seen many violet eyes, and he had mentioned the likeness himself.

Now Marissa understood why they were the same. Soon he would, as well.

The only thing that took away from her excitement was the way he had acted when Joseph had gone to him about Bradley.

She found it hard to believe that Payton James would choose the word of a man like Bradley over that of a man like Joseph McHugh. Joseph would never point an accusing finger at anyone unless he was convinced of that person's guilt.

"He is my father," she whispered to herself. "My *father*."

Although she hated bringing hurt into Joseph's life, she could not help wanting to go to Colonel James.

And then there was Night Wolf. How wonderful it was that he had come into her life. And soon she would be his wife. Even the mere whisper of his name as she breathed it across her lips made her feel warm inside. When she thought of their blissful moments together, she had to blush.

He was the first to take her to a place of wondrous joy as their bodies came together as one.

"Night Wolf," she whispered, sighing as she envisioned him being with her, his hands on her breasts . . .

She lurched as she suddenly found her way blocked by Bradley Coomer. He stepped out from behind the dense cover of golden-leafed aspens, a rifle aimed at her belly.

She drew her steed to a shuddering halt.

"Dismount and come with me," Bradley ordered.

When she didn't budge, he took a step closer. "Don't you try running me down," he said when he saw that she wasn't responding. "I can shoot much faster than that horse can get to me. Now, you don't want to die today, do you? Your father is waiting for you. You want to see your father one last time, don't you?"

"My . . . father?" Marissa gulped, her heart dropping to her toes. "What do you mean? No, don't tell me that you have taken him captive."

"Joseph is waiting for you, so you'd best do as I say, or I'll be taking a dead daughter for him to see before I put a bullet in his heart," Bradley sneered.

"Why are you doing this?" Marissa asked, still unable to move. Her body felt as though it weighed a ton. "Don't you know that you'll be caught? Colonel James will not believe you a second time."

She knew it had been wrong of her to travel alone when Bradley Coomer was still free to do his evil deeds.

If only she had listened to Night Wolf. He would have seen to her safety.

"If you don't get down from that saddle this minute, by damn, I'll shoot you out of it," Bradley said, moving toward her. "Now, wench. Get down from that horse."

Knowing that she must, that he would just as soon shoot her as look at her, Marissa dropped the horse's reins, then slowly slid down to the ground.

When she was standing next to her horse, she felt how weak her knees were from fright. They were actually trembling. But she fought against this fear.

For Joseph, she *had* to stay courageous. She wanted to be taken to him to see if he was all right.

"You and your father have interfered in my future," Bradley growled. "I have no choice but to silence the both of you. It will be no great loss. You are part squaw. It will be good riddance once you are dead."

He motioned with a nod of his head. "Come on, Marissa," he said, stepping closer to her, then standing aside. "Get ahead of me. Go on. Your father is waiting for you."

He laughed cynically. "Father and daughter dead in the same grave," he said. "You'll be joined together for eternity."

Marissa stumbled as she stepped around him, then started walking, her captor following behind her.

Tears welled in her eyes as she thought of her father, Joseph, somewhere, possibly already harmed and waiting to die.

But she had to keep her head. She must stop crying and think of a way to get the best of Bradley. She stopped.

Time. She needed time. She had to come up with a way to trick him.

"What do you think you're doing?" Bradley hissed. He shoved the cold steel of the rifle into her back. "You'd best move onward or I'll shoot you right here, then go and finish your father off. I wanted to see your eyes as you both waited to be killed. I wanted you to beg for mercy together. But if you want to play stubborn, so be it. I can change my plans without blinking an eye."

Realizing that he would kill her before she got to see her father for the last time, Marissa gave Bradley a cold stare over her shoulder, then continued walking.

"You won't get away with this," she said stubbornly. "My true father—Colonel Payton

James—won't believe you are innocent a second time."

Bradley laughed sarcastically. "What did you just say?" he said. "Did I hear you call Payton your father? Have I scared you silly, or what?"

"I was frightened at first," Marissa said. "But now I only pity you. What you heard me say about my father being Colonel James is true. I just discovered that my mother is a full-blood Chippewa woman. I am proud to say that I am part Chippewa."

Bradley reached for Marissa's arm and swung her around to face him. "You might be Chippewa, but you are certainly not the daughter of Colonel Payton James," he said. He narrowed his eyes angrily. "I'm glad I'm going to shut you up for good. I'd hate to think that you'd dirty the name of Colonel James with such lies. Why on earth would you invent such a tale as that? To get back at him for not believing you when you and your father accused me? Well, I'll make certain you can't do that to Colonel James. You deserve to die. Do you hear? You deserve to die!"

Marissa felt an icy dread fill her veins. She had just overplayed her hand. He did not want to wait to kill her any longer. She started walking slowly away from him.

"You're scared now, aren't you?" Bradley taunted as he moved closer to her. "You'll die scared, Marissa, because I'm going to kill—"

He didn't get the chance to say anything else. Suddenly he and Marissa were surrounded by many Indians on horseback, Night Wolf in the lead.

"Drop the firearm or die," Night Wolf ordered, aiming his rifle at Bradley's gut. Although he kept his eyes on Bradley, he spoke to Marissa. "Marissa, I could not allow you to go alone to the fort. I had to come and make certain you were all right."

"Thank God you did," Marissa breathed, aware that Bradley still held her at bay with his rifle, his finger on the trigger. "Be careful, Night Wolf. This man is crazy."

"White man, you can see the firearms and arrows ready to down you. Drop the rifle and step away from Marissa," Night Wolf said, edging his horse closer to Bradley. "Slowly lower the rifle, then drop it."

"Never!" Bradley shouted. He wheeled around to shoot Night Wolf, but Night Wolf was too quick. He fired first.

The rifle rolled out of Bradley's hand as he slowly crumpled.

He landed on his knees, grabbing at his

bloody gut, his eyes on Marissa as she ran to Night Wolf, who had dismounted.

"Night Wolf, oh, Night Wolf, had you waited another moment to arrive, I would be dead," Marissa cried as she flung herself into his arms. "I had said too much. He—he had planned to take me to my father, then kill us both."

She stepped quickly back from Night Wolf. Her eyes were suddenly wild. "Oh, no," she cried. "If Bradley dies, I'll never know where he took my father."

Bradley laughed throatily, then keeled over, facefirst. His eyes were locked in a death stare as he landed awkwardly on the ground, his body twisted strangely.

"No!" Marissa screamed, running to him. She started to drop to her knees, but stopped when she saw Joseph limping out of the forest. His eyes widened when he saw her there, unharmed.

"Daughter!" Joseph cried, embracing her. They clung to one another. "I did not think that we would ever see one another again. That man is insane."

"Father, you're all right! I thought—" she sobbed.

"I found him tied and gagged," Night Wolf said. "He told me what Bradley had planned. I left some of my warriors with your father, then came to find you."

"Thank you, Night Wolf," Marissa said, slowly easing out of her father's arms. She looked down at Bradley and shivered. "Thank God he's dead. He can't hurt anyone ever again."

Joseph smiled at Night Wolf. "Yes, because of Night Wolf, he's dead and we are both very much alive," he said, his voice breaking. "Thank you, Night Wolf. Thank you."

Then Joseph went to Night Wolf and peered intently into his eyes. "What can I do to repay you? It's like a miracle that you came when you did, or—or—both my daughter and I would have died."

"Father?"

Marissa's voice drew Joseph around. She reached for his hands and he twined his fingers through hers.

"I know how you can repay him and make me very happy at the same time. Wish me and Night Wolf well, for we are going to be married. Please give us your blessing," she pleaded.

Joseph was silent for a moment as he gazed deeply into his daughter's violet eyes. Then he swept her into his arms. "My darling daughter," he said. "Yes, I give you my blessing. I want nothing but your happiness. If that means you marry an Indian, so be it."

She hugged him tightly. "Thank you, Father." She stepped away from him again, while holding his hands. "I have so much to say to you. I discovered my true parents—my birth mother and father."

She saw how pale those words made him. She saw his eyes waver.

She embraced him again. "It changes nothing between us. You will forever be my father—the man who held me on his lap when I was a small child and read me books. The man who was everything to me. I do love you so much. I always will."

Joseph held her for a moment longer, then stepped away. He gazed into her eyes, the violet color reminding him that she was not his birth child. "Tell me. I'm listening."

She looked past him and saw the Cree and Chippewa warriors watching and listening. She looked at Night Wolf. She held her hand out for him. "Please join us as I tell my father everything I learned today. I want to do this where there is some privacy. We can stand beside the river as we talk."

Marissa walked between Joseph and Night Wolf, each holding a hand. When they reached the river, she stepped away from them and turned to face her father.

She watched his expression as she told him everything. He was dumbstruck by the truth about her birth father, and the news that her mother was still in the area and had gladly claimed her.

"Payton is your father?" he finally said. "He had an affair and then turned his back on her?"

"Yes, but it was before he knew anything about her being pregnant," Marissa said. "He never knew. I was going to tell him, but, Father, now I'm not sure if I should. I saw your reaction. Lord, what might his be?"

Joseph placed his hands on her shoulders. "Marissa, you must tell him. It's time for the truth to be revealed. Even I would like to know Payton's version of what happened those long years ago."

"Are you saying that you might not believe my mother's story?" Marissa asked.

"I didn't say that," Joseph said, dropping his hands. He kneaded his brow. "It's just that this is almost too much for me to comprehend, much less—"

"Father, it's true," Marissa said. "All of it. My mother carried it around inside her heart all of these years. She would not fabricate anything like this. Colonel James is my birth father, yet he never knew about me. Should he now, Father? Should he?"

"Yes, let's go and talk with him," Joseph said. "Now."

Marissa turned to Night Wolf. "Will you please go with us?" she asked. "You don't have to go inside as we all talk, but please just be there for me?"

"I am always here for you," Night Wolf said, welcoming her into his warm embrace.

He gazed at Joseph over Marissa's shoulder and saw the uneasiness in the white man's eyes. He understood. Much had been revealed to him today, even how much his daughter loved a red man.

Ay-uh, it was a lot to accept all at once. In a sense, he had lost his daughter twice in one day—once to her birth father and once to a red man.

Chapter 34

Night Wolf waited outside the fort while Joseph and Marissa went inside. They held hands as they went into Colonel Payton James's office. He rose from his chair behind his desk when he saw them, his eyebrows arched as he sensed something distinctly different in their behavior.

His jaw tightened, for he could only associate their behavior with Bradley. They had returned to point an accusing finger at the young major again. He was ready to fight them if need be.

"So spit it out," Payton said, angrily folding his arms across his chest. "But know that I still don't believe that Bradley is guilty of anything."

"Bradley isn't the reason we are here," Joseph said, though he knew that Bradley would be a part of the conversation soon. Joseph had decided to bring Bradley's body later, after Payton learned he was Marissa's father.

"Then why have you come?" Payton asked, sitting down on the edge of his desk. He nodded toward the chairs. "Sit. Then we'll talk."

Marissa and Joseph unclasped their hands and sat down beside one another.

They exchanged troubled glances, then Joseph told Payton everything. He explained how they had discovered Marissa's birth mother, and then the truth about Payton being her father.

Payton moved slowly from the desk, his face ashen. He looked carefully at Marissa, who studied him in return with wide eyes.

The eyes. Yes, her eyes were identical to his.

And her hair? He recalled how only recently he had watched her ride away on her horse, her long, thick black hair flying in the breeze. It had reminded him of his lost love.

In that respect, she was the image of Soft Voice. Her mother.

"What are you saying?" Payton gasped.

"You are my father, and Soft Voice is my mother," Marissa answered. "When you broke off your relations with my mother, she was with child. She was shamed in the eyes of her people because there was proof that the child could not be her husband's. And then, when I was born and my skin was white, she knew that no one could know, or she would have been twice shamed. She gave birth to me alone in the forest, then chose to leave me for someone to find. That person was my—my—the man who I have always thought was my father."

Payton's knees almost buckled as he walked slowly back to the chair behind his desk and fell into it. His body seemed so heavy.

"I loved her so much," he said. "But . . ."

"But you loved your career more than her," Joseph finished. "Payton, I know why you left your post at Fort Harris all those years ago. The temptation of the woman you loved being so close might have made you do things that could have jeopardized your standing in the military."

"Yes, but I never forgot her," Payton said, tears shining in his eyes. He looked again at Marissa. "You are my daughter?"

"There is no doubt that I am," Marissa said. "How do you feel about it?"

She wondered if he would take the cowardly way out again and flee his post—and her. But the important thing was that she had discovered the truth and could now go on with her life. All she wanted was to marry the man she loved.

She gazed at Payton at length, trying to feel something for him. However, all she felt was a quiet pity. He had given up the love of a wonderful woman to live the lonesome life of a military man.

"How do I feel?" Payton said. He looked at Marissa again, then to Joseph. "How do *you* feel, Joseph?"

"I'm proud of my daughter," Joseph responded. He reached over and took one of Marissa's hands. "I was afraid the day would come when she would learn the truth. I was prepared for it. I see that she was, as well. She's a woman who has mature feelings about everything. She is someone you should be proud to call daughter, Payton."

"I am," Payton said, rising and going around to stand before Marissa. "Marissa, I guess you know that I feel overwhelmed. Yet I want you to know that I am proud that you are my daughter."

He gestured toward her. "I—I—would like to hug you," he said, his voice breaking. "Will you allow it?"

Marissa swallowed hard. She gave Joseph a questioning look.

He nodded, letting her know that he understood that she had to accept another man as her true father. She got slowly to her feet and moved into Payton's arms.

"My daughter," Payton said, holding her endearingly. "Marissa, my life has been so lonely. I made so many mistakes. But when I turned my back on the woman I loved, I unknowingly turned my back on you. I'm sorry, Marissa. Damn sorry."

"I can tell that you are," Marissa said soothingly. She wanted to feel something as he held her, yet she again felt nothing but a strange sort of pity. She continued to hug him, though. He seemed to need it.

When he eased away from her, she saw tears streaming from his eyes. She realized that he had so many regrets, and she started to feel more empathy for him. She began to have feelings that until now had only belonged to another father.

"I was wrong those long years ago," Payton said, sitting behind his desk again. "I've lived a lonely life. I've missed Soft Voice with all my heart. But after I turned my back on her, I saw no way of ever going back. I believed that she had made things right with her husband and had probably had many children by him."

"The truth is that she lived a lonely life without a husband or her child," Marissa said. "She would like to see you. She forgave you long ago. She has always loved you."

"After what I did she still loves me?" Payton asked. "She wants to see me?"

"You are a high-ranking officer in the military. You know that you don't want to give that up. I don't think it would be wise of you to go. You would only hurt her again."

Payton raked his fingers through his hair. "I'm bored to death with the military. If I could start all over again, I would do so many things differently. I would never turn my back on a love like the love I had with Soft Voice."

"Are you saying you will give up the military for her?" Joseph asked, his eyes widening.

"If Soft Voice will have me, yes, that's exactly what I'm saying," Payton said hoarsely. "I'll retire in a minute and marry Soft Voice. We can settle elsewhere in our own private world."

Then Payton gave Joseph a glance. "I'll see to it that Bradley moves up, hopefully into my position here at Fort Harris."

"You'll what?" Joseph said, jumping up from the chair. He doubled his hands into fists at his sides. "After what I told you about that son of a bitch, you'd still recommend him to be in charge at Fort Harris?"

"Joseph, I told you how I felt," Payton grumbled. "I would never believe that lie in a million years. Bradley would be risking too much to try anything as stupid as that."

Marissa leapt to her feet beside Joseph. "Bradley is responsible for more than trying to assault that lovely Indian woman," she blurted out. "We were waiting to tell you about what happened until you knew about me and my mother."

"What are you talking about?" Payton asked, rising slowly. "What happened?"

"Bradley is dead," Joseph said solemnly.

Both Joseph and Marissa watched Payton flinch as though he had been shot, then turn pale. He looked at them disbelievingly.

"Dead?" he asked, his voice barely a whisper.

Joseph told Payton what had happened. Payton looked bewildered.

"I didn't know him at all," Payton said. "He had me completely fooled."

"He was a worthless coward," Joseph said.

Payton looked from Joseph to Marissa. "I feel so foolish, so very, very foolish," he said, his voice breaking.

"You wanted to believe that there was good in the young man," Joseph said, going to sit on the edge of the desk close to Payton. "You wanted to help him because you saw yourself in him when you were younger. But you weren't like him at all, Payton. You have morals. You have a heart. Now you have more than that. You have a daughter, and a woman who is waiting to see you regardless of what you did those many years ago."

Payton went to Marissa. "Will you take me to your mother?"

She peered up into the eyes that were so much like her own, then took his hand. "Yes, I'll take you to her."

He looked quickly at Joseph. "Where is Bradley?"

"You go on with Marissa. I'll see to it that Bradley's body is brought to the fort while you are gone," Joseph urged. "Payton, don't think about that man and how he duped you. It's just like you to see only the good in someone. Be proud of that trait."

Payton gave Joseph a hug. "I'm lucky to have known you for so long and to have such a friend as you. I hope knowing that I'm Marissa's father won't create a strain between us."

"It won't," Joseph said, smiling at Marissa. "I think that sweet thing has enough love to share with both of us."

Marissa smiled, flicked tears from her eyes, and nodded. "Yes, I do," she said as she thought of someone else.

"I've more to tell you," she said, looking Payton directly in the eye.

"What else could there be?" he asked.

"I'm going to be getting married soon," she said.

"You are getting married?" Payton repeated in surprise. "Who? You were planning on marrying Bradley. Who else has been courting you that I didn't know about?"

"I'm going to marry Chief Night Wolf," Marissa said, watching his expression for his reaction.

"Chief Night Wolf?" Payton repeated. "How did this happen?"

"I'll tell you on our way to the Cree village," Marissa said, hooking an arm through Payton's. "Come on. Let's go. Night Wolf is just outside the fort's walls waiting for us. He will accompany us to the village."

"My head is spinning," Payton said, laughing lightly as Joseph walked with them out of the office.

"So is mine," Joseph chuckled. "But things are good, right?"

"Very," Payton said, glancing at Marissa. "Yes, very, very good."

She gave him a radiant smile.

Chapter 35

Marissa and Night Wolf stood apart from Soft Voice and Payton as they saw each other for the first time in eighteen years. Marissa could tell that Payton was taken aback by Soft Voice's appearance. She looked much older than her years because of her unhappiness and loneliness.

Soft Voice was surprised that Payton had not aged much in her eyes. She still saw his handsomeness and smiled shyly at him.

"I am so sorry," Payton said, then swept Soft Voice into his arms. "I don't know how I could have left you. I have never stopped thinking about you. Never."

Soft Voice sobbed. "I have never forgotten you," she said, clinging to him. "My dreams were filled with you. Memories of you are what kept me alive. Otherwise I would have died long ago."

"You had a child—*our* child," Payton said, his voice breaking. "You never told me."

"Would things have changed?" Soft Voice asked, leaning away from him and looking up into his eyes. "Would you have chosen me and our child over the military?"

Payton's eyes wavered. "Please don't ask," he said. "I was such an ambitious young man. But were it now, and you came to me with child, I would quickly turn my back on the military."

His eyes lowered. "I was wrong," he said softly. "I have been a lonely man. Such a lonely man."

"Your ambitions blinded you to what was best in life," Soft Voice said, closing her eyes in ecstasy as Payton gently smoothed a tear away from her cheek. "I understood your ambition. You were such a handsome man in your uniform."

She slowly opened her eyes. "As you are even now," she murmured.

"Can you ever forgive me?" Payton asked. "Can you accept me now in your life? I never, ever forgot you. I want to start over again with you. I want to be your husband. I—I—want to be a father to our child."

Marissa covered her mouth as she choked on a sob, touched by what was happening before her eyes. She saw the love that her mother and father had for one another. It was so sad, though, that all of those years were wasted, even though they loved each other so much.

She waited anxiously for her mother's response. She wanted them to come together again and make up for all the years that were lost to them.

She smiled warmly at Night Wolf as his hand slid into hers. He pulled her closer to him. "Maybe they need privacy," he whispered to her.

"Let's wait just a moment longer," Marissa whispered back. "I want to hear what Mother says."

Night Wolf squeezed her hand affectionately. "Yes, we will wait," he said, watching the two lovers. He could not help feel strange about seeing an Indian woman in the arms of a military man. Although Marissa's skin was white, and she was going to be his wife, it seemed different somehow.

But he knew that was exactly where the problem arose. Soft Voice had fallen in love with a man in uniform. Had he been just an ordinary citizen of the white world, it would have not been so hard for them to be together all those years ago.

As it was, the military was there purposely

to protect whites against people of red skin. He understood why Payton had denied himself such a love, for back then, even more than now, it was forbidden in the eyes of both the red and the white communities.

But now it seemed that things were going to be all right between the two. And Marissa was going to have her parents to love, and to be loved by.

Ay-uh, it did seem that things were going to be righted today. The only one who might feel left out was the one who had taken Marissa in and brought her up as his own.

But he knew that Marissa would not allow that to happen. She loved Joseph McHugh with every fiber of her being. She would never turn her back on him.

"I want you. Oh, how badly I want you, Payton, but—but what of your career?" Soft Voice asked. "How could I be a part of your life while you are still an officer for the United States cavalry? I could never live among those who are under your command at the fort. I would feel out of place. The men at the fort would feel awkward in my presence. What of your career if you say you want me back in your life?"

"Like I said, Soft Voice, it has been a lonesome, empty life for me," Payton said. "Yes, I am proud of what I have achieved for our country. But I am sorely tired of it all now. I wish only for a life of peace and harmony—and love. I will gladly discard my uniform and my title as colonel if it means that I can have you in my life again, and our daughter. I will resign my post. I shall leave the military."

"You will do that for me?" Soft Voice asked, her eyes filling with tears again.

"Yes, I will do that for you," Payton said, placing a gentle hand on her copper face. "And also for our daughter. We shall have a life together as a family. I shall build us a cabin not far from your village. We shall have a garden. We shall have everything we have not yet had together. We shall be man and wife—father and mother."

Sobbing, Soft Voice flung herself into his arms. "I have waited so long for this," she cried. "I did not think it could happen. My dreams, my prayers to *Wenebojo*, have come true. *Ay-uh*, Payton, I want us to be married. I want a home with you. I want a garden. I want a place where our daughter and her husband can come and visit us. I want a place for our grandchildren to come and play and be happy!"

"Grandchildren," Payton said almost dreamily. "Yes, grandchildren!"

Marissa tugged on Night Wolf's hand and

encouraged him to leave Soft Voice's tepee with her.

Once outside, she hugged him. "I am so happy," she cried. "I am so happy for them, and for myself. I have not only one father but two, and a wonderful, caring mother. And my father is giving up everything he has always known to make things right for her. It's so wonderful, Night Wolf."

"I believe they are happy about thoughts of grandchildren," Night Wolf said, gazing down into Marissa's eyes. "Should not we make grandchildren for them as quickly as possible?"

"Are you saying—"

"I am saying let them have these moments alone, as we should go and have our own," Night Wolf said, his eyes twinkling. "Let us go and make love, Marissa, and talk of a day when we can speak our vows."

"Do you think that my mother and father might speak their vows on the same day we speak ours?" Marissa said excitedly. "Would not that just be too perfect?"

"I am certain they would agree to such a plan as that," Night Wolf said, holding her hand and walking with her toward his tepee.

"I don't want Joseph ever to feel left out of

our lives," she said as he held the entrance flap back for her.

"We will make certain of that," Night Wolf said, closing the flap and tying it to ensure their privacy.

"My love," Marissa sighed, going to him. Their lips came together, their bodies pressed hungrily against each other.

Chapter 36

"Soon, my woman, we will be making love as man and wife," Night Wolf whispered against Marissa's lips as he moved over her with his muscled body, molding himself perfectly to the curved hollow of her hips.

She shivered with ecstasy and clung to his neck as he pressed gently into her yielding folds, then deeper as she spread her legs apart.

"My husband," Marissa whispered back, breathless as he thrust rhythmically within her. "I shall savor saying that word over and over again. My *husband*."

He pressed his lips against hers, his hands moving down her body until they cupped her buttocks.

Their naked flesh fused, flesh against flesh, heart against heart.

Marissa melted beneath his heated kiss. She felt herself floating, with a spiraling need more intense than before.

She moved her body sinuously against his, matching his rhythm. Her breath caught in her throat as he seemed to go more deeply and touch something wonderful inside her.

He kissed her more urgently as she arched toward him. With a groan he pulled her against him. He had never been so inflamed with longing. Everything within him seemed fluid with fire, and as they moved together each moment brought him more bliss, more joy.

His hands reached for hers, then he twined his fingers through hers as he held her hands above her head.

"My love," Marissa whispered, surges of ecstasy welling within her. "I cannot hold back any longer. The pleasure, ah, the pleasure is so intense, so—"

He kissed her again, stealing her words away, each kiss bringing up fresh desire.

Tremors cascaded down Night Wolf's body.

He made one last plunge into her, then threw his head back and closed his eyes as he spilled his seed within her and her body shook in unison with his.

They both lay on their backs beside the fire, their bodies gleaming beneath the flames that cast dancing shadows upon them.

Marissa leaned up on an elbow when she

heard laughter outside, not far from Night Wolf's lodge.

"I want many children," she whispered. "I have three parents now to love our children. It will be a wonderful time for us now that everyone is at peace."

"The father who raised you?" Night Wolf asked. "Do you think he will be able to share you with your true father and mother? Or do you think there will be jealousy among them?"

"Joseph is a gentle, fair, and loving man. I don't expect him to be jealous, especially since he knows that his childhood friend is my true father," Marissa answered. "This will bring them closer together."

"And do you feel as wonderful about all of this as your voice and eyes seem to show?" Night Wolf asked, placing a gentle hand on her cheek. "You do seem to have a sense of peace about you that came with the discovery of who you truly are."

"I am at peace. But it is not only because I have discovered my true heritage," Marissa said, snuggling closer against his naked body. "It is because of you that there is joy in my eyes. Had I not been able to have your love, I would have been left only half a woman."

"As I would have been only half a man,"

Night Wolf said, brushing soft kisses across her lips.

They stretched out on their backs together and looked through the smoke hole overhead. They gazed at the star-speckled sky.

"Legend says the large bright stars are wise old warriors and the small dim ones are handsome young braves," Night Wolf explained. "Those stars that are clustered together and look like an animal are buffalo that have gotten away during our spring hunt."

"Are you eager for the hunt?" Marissa asked.

"It is an exciting time of year for us warriors," Night Wolf said, smiling at her. "I am always eager to see the great herds of big-shouldered buffalo. The buffalo is an elder, a master, medicine, food, fire, and prayer. Buffalo is our everything."

There was more laughter outside the lodge, this time much louder.

"I think my nephew is playing marbles again, and I imagine he is winning, as he usually does," Night Wolf said, sitting up, looking toward the closed entrance flap.

"Marbles?" Marissa said, arching an eyebrow. "I used to play marbles with friends in Kansas City. I was teased for being a tomboy, but I could beat everyone at a game of marbles."

"I brought several home from your father's trading post for Little Moon," Night Wolf said. "He shared them with his best friends."

"Possibly because he thought he would be winning them back," Marissa said, laughing softly.

"Perhaps," Night Wolf said, chuckling.

He reached for his breechclout. "I would like to see you challenge Little Moon to a game of marbles," he said, sliding his breechclout up his legs, until it was secure.

"You would?" she asked, noticing how quickly he had dressed. "Now? You want me to do it now?"

"It is a fun night, so, *ay-uh*, let me see you challenge my nephew," Night Wolf said, handing Marissa's clothes to her. "Are you game?"

"Am I game?" Marissa said, smiling at his use of a phrase used in the white community. "Certainly I am game."

She hurried into her clothes and boots, then stepped outside with Night Wolf.

They walked over to where Little Moon and his friends were playing close to the light of the fire.

Night Wolf placed a hand on his nephew's shoulder.

"Marissa wishes to challenge you," Night Wolf said, casting Marissa a playful glance.

"She does?" Little Moon said, his eyes widening as he looked at Marissa.

"I would enjoy it if you would," Marissa said, waiting to sit among the circle of young braves who were looking at her with interest.

"Come," Little Moon said, gesturing with a hand as he scooted over and made room for Marissa.

As Night Wolf stood behind her, Marissa sat down between Little Moon and another young brave.

She noticed that they did not know the rules of the game. There was no circle, and they did not know how to shoot the marbles accurately.

She reached for a stick that lay beyond the burning fire, and drew a circle in the dirt as she explained why. She set several marbles in the circle, then chose a red-striped one to show Little Moon and the others how to position their fingers in order to shoot properly.

When the marble she shot clicked hard against another one, the young braves squealed with delight. Each tried positioning his fingers as Marissa had shown them.

Soon they were shooting marble after marble, giggling as they discovered the way to win the game, even against Little Moon.

But the merriment came to a quick halt when the sound of approaching horses caused everyone to rise to their feet and watch the outer perimeter of the village.

Marissa stood at Night Wolf's side as several men came into view and rode toward him. There was only one Indian warrior among the men. The rest were white and dressed as civilians.

Blue Star came to stand beside Night Wolf. She seemed interested in those arriving beneath the moonlight. Then she squealed and ran toward one of the men.

The stranger grabbed Blue Star, pulled her up onto his lap and kissed her.

Brave Hawk came to Night Wolf's side. "I cannot believe what I am seeing," he said.

"Who is that?" Night Wolf asked, watching Blue Star and her joy at being with the white man.

"Father Scott Taylor," Brave Hawk said. "He has followed my sister here. He no longer wears the robe of a priest. He seems to have given it up for my sister."

He glanced at the warrior who had led Scott Taylor and his men to the village. "The warrior is a guide that I know," he said. "He was aware of where we were settling. Taylor must have asked him to lead him here. He could not stay away from my sister."

Marissa eavesdropped on Brave Hawk's conversation with Night Wolf. She was surprised that things worked out so wonderfully for Blue Star.

Night Wolf took Marissa by the hand and walked with her to the white men, who were now dismounting.

"Welcome," he said, extending a hand to one of them.

"We have accompanied Scott Taylor to your village to make certain he arrived safely," the one sandy-haired man said. "We would like to spend the night, then head back to Minnesota country in the morning."

"You are welcome to stay as long as you wish," Night Wolf said.

Blue Star leapt from Taylor's lap and beamed at him as he dismounted. She grabbed him by a hand and led him over to Night Wolf.

"Night Wolf, this is Scott Taylor," she said, the excitement still in her voice. "He was a priest, but he is no longer. He has come to marry me instead."

Scott Taylor smiled at Night Wolf and offered him a hand of friendship. "I heard a lot about you before Blue Star left for your village. I was afraid I would arrive too late. I thought you might be married by now." He smiled widely. "I am glad that I was wrong."

"Night Wolf is marrying Marissa," Blue Star said, smiling at Marissa.

Marissa returned the smile. "I am so happy for you."

"I am happy for myself, too," Blue Star said, again smiling up at Scott. "Scott, I still cannot believe you are here. I thought I would be living a lonesome life. Now I will not ever be lonely again."

Scott placed an arm around her waist and drew her closer to him. "I could not stay away," he said, his voice breaking as he looked at Brave Hawk. "I could not see life without your sister, Brave Hawk. I knew after she was gone that my love was for her, not for my religion. I left my robes behind me. I shall wear them no more."

"To love me this much?" Blue Star said, gazing into Scott's deep blue eyes. "To be loved this much?"

"Yes, to be loved this much," Scott said, smiling down at her. "I do love you very much."

"I love you, too," Blue Star murmured.

"Come and sit beside the outdoor fire. The food will be brought to us," Night Wolf said, gesturing toward the fire.

Soft Voice emerged from her tepee with Payton, their hands clasped. Night Wolf's mother and Moon Song joined the large crowd that was quickly assembling around the fire.

After everyone was sitting on blankets and food was being sent around the large circle, Night Wolf and Marissa took a blanket and sneaked away into the night.

The moon reflected its white sheen onto the water as Night Wolf took the corners of the blanket and enveloped them together beneath it.

"My love, what I have just done with the blanket signifies the marriage bond between us," he said as he smiled down at her. "Tomorrow the ceremony will finalize that bond."

"Tomorrow?" Marissa said, her eyes wide.

"*Ay-uh*, tomorrow," he said, making sure the blanket did not fall away as he pulled Marissa closer, her breasts crushed against his powerful chest.

Their lips came together in a long, deep kiss.

"Tomorrow," he whispered against her lips.

Epilogue

It was *wahbegvone-geezis*, the moon of the flowers. Snow still huddled in the coulees, shrinking daily beneath the warm rays of the sun. Outside of the Cree village, on the nearby hillsides, pussy willows proudly displayed their furry coats, while delicate crocuses cast colorful patches of purple amid the dry, brown prairie grass.

Married for five winters, and content as Night Wolf's wife, Marissa was alone in her lodge, preparing to do beadwork beside the firepit. She untied the long-tasseled strings that bound her small brown buckskin sewing bag and spilled the colored beads upon a mat beside her. She smoothed out a double sheet of soft white doeskin on a lapboard, and drew a long, narrow blade from a beaded case that hung on the left of her wide belt. She carefully trimmed the doeskin into the shape she preferred.

She laid the vest pattern across her folded legs. Marissa chose to make an outline of red upon a background of myrtle green, and from a skein of finely twisted threads of silvery sinews, she pulled out a single one.

With an awl she pierced the doeskin and skillfully threaded it with white sinew. Picking up the tiny beads, one by one, she strung them with the point of her thread, careful to twist it after every stitch. While placing the beads on the vest that her husband would wear at special celebrations, Marissa became lost in thought.

That first winter as Night Wolf's wife, she had learned that winter and blizzards were as much a part of the Indian's life as were the pleasant days of summer. When the wind howled, it sounded like sorrowful packs of wolves, and when the wolves howled, it sounded like mournful cries of the wind.

But no matter how cold it became, or how strong the winds blew, the Cree and Chippewa people stayed warm in their homes of stretched buffalo hides. They often gathered around fires, drinking broth made from buffalo marrow as stories were told and warriors reminisced.

As the men talked, the women would repair their husbands' leather shirts, finish some intricate quillwork on a dress or moccasins, or teach a girl child a variety of beadwork stitches.

And then there was the dark side of winter. When the people ran short of firewood, the young braves would collect buffalo chips. The chips often burned too quickly unless their mothers had a bit of fat to suspend above the fire to slowly drip onto the dung, making it last longer and create better heat.

Marissa was surprised that on the coldest mornings, Night Wolf would strip to his breechclout and go outside to rub snow on his body.

Trim, fit, and hardened by a life in the outdoors, Night Wolf had adjusted long ago to the cold and could easily withstand the rigors of the trail.

Marissa smiled over the many memories from living among her husband's people, who were now her own. She could no longer envision herself living anywhere else.

Her heart warmed at the thought of her two fathers, both whom she loved so much. And her mother. Oh, how she loved her. It was as though Marissa had never been away from her. Her closeness to Soft Voice had become so endearing. Although her mother no longer lived in the village, she was not all that far away.

Payton had retired from the military and built his wife a lovely four-room cabin halfway between the village and Fort Harris. He continued to work at the fort as an advisor and interpreter when Indians visiting from distant tribes came to meet with the new colonel. Even though he had married an Indian maiden, he was no less respected than when he was a powerful colonel.

Marissa also thought about her father, Joseph. His trading post was prosperous, and he now had a young family. He had married the daughter of the new colonel at the fort, and she was nine months pregnant with her first child. Marissa looked forward to her new brother or sister.

And then there were Moon Song and Brave Hawk. They had had a son, who was a delight for Little Moon, who had always prayed that one day he would have a brother.

There was even her own family to glory over. Her and Night Wolf's dream of having many children had begun nine months after their wedding night. Twin sons were born to them. Until their vision quests, when they would receive their warrior names, they were called One Wolf and Two Wolf. One Wolf had intense violet eyes and light copper skin, while Two Wolf had the eyes and skin of his father.

"My sons," Marissa whispered, the voices of her children carrying to her as they played with others their same age. The spring sunshine had lured the restless boys outside after they had been cooped up in the tepee during those long, cold winter months.

She laughed to herself when she heard Two Wolf's voice, filled with authority, rising above the others. Two Wolf seemed to have become a leader. The others followed him as they played or mock-hunted, as though it were his destiny to lead, not follow.

Marissa had wondered if that meant Two Wolf would step into chieftainship later on in life, or if One Wolf would challenge him.

"I don't even want to think about that," she said to herself.

Instead, she thought of Little Moon teaching her sons how to play marbles. Each now had a bag of his own. Their grandfather made certain that they had brightly colored marbles to trade with the other children.

Her smile broadened when she thought of the next change in her life. Another child. She was big with child, and she somehow knew that this child would be a daughter. She had not chosen a name yet, afraid that might jinx things.

She chose a porcupine quill that she had

dyed a soft green to sew on the vest, along with the beads. The sharp points were poisonous and would work into the flesh, so she cut off the prickly end and burned it before working it into the design on the vest. She dipped the rest of the quill into a small bowl of water to moisten it, then flattened it between the nails of her thumbs and forefingers.

Footsteps approaching the tepee drew her eyes to the entrance flap. Her husband's hand lifted the flap, before he stepped inside. The same thrill she had felt the first time she saw him raced through her now. She had not known that loving someone could be this intense and this *ah-pah-nay*, forever, but loving Night Wolf was that and more. Their relationship was *mee-kah-wah-diz-ee*, beautiful.

"*Ee-quay*, wife, I see you are enjoying yourself this evening," he said, glancing toward the waning fire, then at Marissa.

When he saw the bead of sweat above her lip, he went outside and pulled the wooden pegs that pinned the skirt of the tepee to the ground, then rolled the buffalo hide part way up on the pole frame.

As he stepped inside again, Marissa enjoyed the cool evening breeze sweeping freely through the dwelling, and the perfume of sweet grasses and wildflowers from the prairie and forests wafting into the lodge.

"*Mee-gway-chee-wahn-dum*, thank you, darling." She sighed with pleasure as he bent before her and gently wiped the perspiration away from her upper lip. "I was so absorbed in my beadwork, I had not noticed how warm I had become."

Nigh Wolf smiled and placed a gentle hand on her belly. "Has the child kicked today?"

"So much it has been hard to keep my lapboard in place," Marissa said, giggling. "When I finish this vest, do not be surprised to see a footprint or a knee print or two on it."

"You have sewn enough today, my *ee-quay*," he said, removing everything from her lap and laying it aside on the floor mats.

He took her gently by the hand. "*Mah-bee-szhon*, come," he urged. "We shall go outside and watch the sunset together. It is the most *mee-kah-wah-diz-ee*, beautiful, time of the year. It was made for you, who are just as *mee-kah-wah-diz-ee*."

Even though Marissa was used to his compliments, she blushed and smiled at him as he helped her up from the floor. "You spoil me, you know."

"*Gah-ween*, no, what I do is not called spoiling, it is called loving," Night Wolf said, sliding an arm around her waist, then stepping outside into the magical time of evening.

They paused to look at their sons at play. Their marbles were back in their bags, and for the moment their game had turned into hide-and-seek.

One Wolf was eagerly searching for Two Wolf, and squealed when he found him hunkered behind a stack of firewood.

"I found you!" One Wolf said, giggling when Two Wolf playfully wrestled him to the ground.

"They are content, those sons of ours," Night Wolf said, walking with Marissa away from the play area to the water's edge, where the canoes were moored.

"As we are," Marissa murmured, leaning into his embrace as they stood side by side, gazing up at the sky. "Just look at it, Night Wolf. Have you ever seen a sunset as lovely as this evening's?"

"Never," Night Wolf said.

The clouds were fringed with flaming pinks that softened to paler tones as light cast over their billowy surface. Streaks of magenta, orange, and yellow swept out from the western horizon, reflecting into the river and coloring the distant hills in purple and blues.

"*Ee-quay*, the Cree believe the spirit of daylight sees everything that happens and hears all that is said during the hours of sunshine and, to let the world know that it is leaving, creates a spectacle such as this evening's sky for everyone to see."

He turned to her and held her hands, his gaze slowly drifting over her. She was wearing doeskin, and the waning light made her look as pale as milk, yet radiant. "The sky might be something wonderful to see after those long, gray skies of winter, but, *ee-quay*, nothing can ever outdo you in radiance. As it was that first time I saw you, looking at you steals my breath away."

"But I am so big with child," Marissa demurred. "How can you see anything radiant in that?"

He gently splayed his fingers across her belly. "How?" he asked. "Because that bigness—that child—is *you*."

Those words melted Marissa's heart. She tried to fling herself into his arms, but realized that was not as easily done when something round and large came between them. She started to laugh.

Night Wolf slid his arms around her and drew her as close as he could under the circumstances. His lips came softly down upon hers in a sweet, lingering kiss. She twined her arms around his neck and became that eighteen-year-old girl all over again who fell in love with a handsome Cree chief. She—

Night Wolf felt Marissa tense, then heard her gasp against his lips. He stepped away from her and gazed at her questioningly.

"It is time," she said, wincing as another pain shot through her abdomen. "Night Wolf, I am having hard, quick labor pains. Our child will be born soon. I can feel it. There is hardly any time to prepare me for it."

Although she was heavy and awkward, he lifted her and hurried away from the river. All eyes were on them when Marissa unsuccessfully tried to stifle a cry of pain.

"Mother!" Night Wolf cried as he hurried onward. *"Mah-bee-szhon*, come! Marissa is ready to have our child!"

His mother came from her tepee, eyes wide, her steps quick. Everyone emerged from the lodges to be a part of their chief and his wife's happy moment.

The twins ran alongside their father, their eyes never leaving their mother.

Then everything seemed to happen all at once.

Marissa was in Yellow Blossom's tepee. Several women stood around Marissa as she lay with her legs spread on a thick layer of blankets.

Night Wolf stood outside with his sons, each child clinging to a separate leg, their eyes eagerly watching the closed entrance flap.

Soon the whole village, both Cree and Chippewa, heard the first cries of a precious little girl, the first daughter born to their chief and his wife.

Yellow Blossom carried the bundle of joy out to Night Wolf and placed her gently in his arms.

He squatted on his haunches so that his sons could see their sister, then stood and held the baby high above his head so that everyone could see her.

"A daughter!" he shouted. "My wife gave birth to a daughter!"

Marissa was so happy she cried. Soon she was cleaned, on fresh blankets, and in a soft doeskin gown. Night Wolf came into the tepee, his daughter so tiny in his massively muscled arms.

Night Wolf gently laid the baby in Marissa's arms.

Together they looked at the pretty white face and eyes as violet as her mother's.

"I have a tiny Marissa now," Night Wolf said, chuckling.

"I am so proud," Marissa said. The entrance flap shoved open as the twins came into the tepee. She reached a hand out, and both came and took hold of it. "You have a sister. Is she not pretty?"

"Pretty like you," One Wolf said, smiling brightly.

"I like my sister," Two Wolf said, reaching a hand to the child's face, softly touching it. "She is so very tiny."

"Yes, tiny and fragile," Marissa said, looking from son to son. "You must be gentle with her. But one day she will be walking and playing with you. She will enjoy her brothers."

Night Wolf smiled as he watched his family. He was glad that he had not gone through with the agreement to marry Blue Star. He would have never known the wonder of now—the wonder of Marissa and their children. No man's contentment could be as deeply felt as was his.

He gazed over at Marissa. They exchanged silent, sweet smiles, for words were unnecessary to describe how they both felt at this moment.

No.

No one's contentment could be as deeply felt as was *theirs*.

Letter to the Reader

Dear Reader:

I hope you enjoyed reading *Night Wolf*. There are many more novels to come in my NAL/ Signet Indian Series. Look for a new book in the stores every six months.

Those of you who are collecting my Indian romances and want to hear more about them and the Cassie Edwards Fan Club can send for my latest newsletter, bookmark, and autographed photograph. For a prompt reply, please send a stamped, self-addressed, legal-sized envelope to:

Cassie Edwards
6709 North Country Club Road
Mattoon, Illinois 61938

You can also visit my Web site at
www.cassieedwards.com

Always,

Cassie Edwards

NOW AVAILABLE IN HARDCOVER

A NOVEL BY THE AUTHOR OF *Picture Maker*

Dream Weaver

PENINA KEEN SPINKA

DUTTON